Snowed in with the Billionaire

Snowed In Series

Can be read in any order

Maya Black

This is a work of fiction. Names, characters, businesses, places, events and incidents are either the products of the author's imagination or used in a fictitious manner. Any resemblance to actual persons, living or dead, or actual events is purely coincidental.

Copyright © 2024 by Maya Black

All rights reserved.

No part of this book may be reproduced in any form or by any electronic or mechanical means, including information storage and retrieval systems, without written permission from the publisher, except for the use of brief quotations in a book review.

If you would like to use material from this book, prior written permission must be obtained by contacting the publisher at:

authormayablack@gmail.com

First edition: January 2025

Contents

Chapter 1	1
Chapter 2	9
Chapter 3	15
Chapter 4	17
Chapter 5	27
Chapter 6	35
Chapter 7	41
Chapter 8	47
Chapter 9	51
Chapter 10	57
Chapter 11	63
Chapter 12	67
Chapter 13	73
Chapter 14	77
Chapter 15	81
Chapter 16	85
Chapter 17	95
Chapter 18	99
Epilogue	117
Join Maya Black's Newsletter	123
About Maya Black	125
Also by Maya Black	127

Millie

MILLIE LEANED FORWARD in her seat and peered through the thick layer of snow that had covered her windshield.

How could the forecast turn out to be so inaccurate?

She was crawling through a real blizzard when all they were expected to get was a couple of inches and a slight breeze. Her back ached from leaning into the windshield to make out the lines on the road, and her shoulders were knotted. She was also chilly. Very chilly. The air that emerged from the heater, which she had battled with prior to leaving the parking lot, was, at most, tepid. Despite her gloves, she could not feel her fingertips.

It was clear from the empty road that everyone else had received the word regarding the change in the forecast, but not her. Not only that, but she was the lone idiot who accepted a job offer on Christmas Eve even though she still had a trip to complete. She had thought of calling off the trip home as the first flakes fell, but her parents expected her to be there, snowstorm or not. She was fighting to drive safely in a dinosaur of a car that could hardly get her to and from work on a good day, all because of their expectations.

Her inability to defrost her windows and the snowstorm meant that her windshield wipers were not keeping up, which made visibility worse. Millie feared that ice would make it harder for her to see.

Was it turning from snow to sleet?

She still had at least two hours of misery left until she pulled into her parent's driveway. Her teeth were chattering and her nose was frozen. She reached her hand over to the tiny knob and turned up the radio's volume. It was among the few items in the car that remained functional.

A few songs in, Millie started to bounce along to the advertisements. The automobile skidded briefly on an especially icy stretch of road, as she reached to change the station because she detested listening to the commercials. Just barely, she was able to get control back before her tires came off the road. After that, she concluded that it wasn't really that big of a deal to listen to ads. She had to operate the vehicle with two hands.

The station turned from commercials to updates on the road and weather reports. Millie's stomach dropped as she listened to the reports. The storm wasn't even close to ending, and the state of the roadways was getting worse.

Had she realized ahead of time how terrible it was going to be, she would have remained home. However, it was now too late. Turning around wouldn't help her because she was getting closer to her destination than her starting place. Additionally, she didn't think she would have any luck attempting to get a room at one of the motels along the road in this kind of weather. Nope, all she could do was keep going and hope for the best. Following the official reports, the radio announcer and his companion joked around about the storm before chatting about rumors.

The female announcer questioned, "Now what do you think of billionaire playboy, Hayden Dickinson?"

The man said in an irritated tone, "I have a lot that I could say about Mr. Dickinson, but I need to keep it clean for our audience, which doesn't leave me with a lot of options."

"Are you jealous?" she asked.

Millie listened intently, eager to hear about the most recent exploits of the not so mysterious rich lad. His adventures seemed to provide unending pleasure, and he was constantly in the spotlight.

"I'm just not a fan," he said. "He comes across as a jerk."

"Don't be so harsh with him." The female chuckled. "He's single, attractive, youthful, and still getting his bearings."

He joked with his co-host, "Wait, you're not one of Haydee boy's groupies, are you?"

"What prevents me from being one? You have to concede that he is a handsome man!"

"Indeed, he has a good appearance. The issue is that he has a tremendous ego since he is aware of it."

"I'm sure there's something really big about him," the woman said. "In any case, I think our favourite bachelor will have an interesting holiday. Look at this: Hayden was leaving his yearly charity Christmas Gala earlier tonight, of course, with an enigmatic blonde on his arm."

Millie rolled her eyes at how predictable the guy was. She didn't give a damn about Hayden Dickinson and wished she could change the station.

"And? That is not new information. He's always with someone."

"No, there's more! Our boy was shot by someone!"

Millie's mouth dropped involuntarily as the woman took a moment to process what she had said. Though she didn't exactly follow the CEO's every step, she also wasn't in favor of his demise. She would much rather he simply mature a little and receive a harsh reality check. The way women put themselves at his feet and he just tossed them aside as he pleased disgusted her.

Was the shooter one of those cast-off women?

Although Millie would never intentionally hurt anyone, the man's actions have to be really bad for someone to pursue him in that way.

"Who fired a shot? Are they deranged? Do people not recognize Hayden Dickinson's immense power?" he questioned, his tone doubtful. "Do they know who the shooter is?"

"Not yet, although there are whispers that it's a business associate who was abandoned. Although Hayden was unharmed, his security team hurried him out of the scene before the throng could comprehend what was happening."

"And now that the attempt on his life has been publicized, I'm sure the internet has crashed from the sheer volume of women distraught over the almost fatal outcome."

The woman reprimanded, "You can't blame us for being a little starstruck by him. He leads an opulent lifestyle. How I would love to spend even a single night or two with him!"

"So, tell me, where's Dickinson now?" the man inquired. "You mentioned that he was led away, but where?"

"As for his whereabouts, there are only rumors," she answered. Some have speculated that he is in protective custody, while others claim he is in a safe place. Since the event, which occurred roughly two hours ago, he has not been seen. He could be anywhere by now."

"I hope old Haydie boy is okay, for you and for all the lonely housewives out there. Wouldn't want to ruin your vacation."

She answered, "Yeah, I hope he's okay, too. However, I doubt he'll allow this minor incident to spoil his vacation, either."

He chuckled. "I'm sure he's secluded himself with a super-model, using his candy cane in an inventive manner."

Millie furrowed her brow. Now it was just starting to get annoying, enough that she seized the opportunity to reach over and turn the knob to the off position. With all the conversation, she was unable to focus while driving. Besides, she wasn't interested in following the rumors about Hayden Dickinson.

As her car crawled through the snow with the radio off, she became aware of how stressed the engine was. She was starting to question why she was even going on this trip in the first place as the gears were grinding. If she failed to show up, it was unlikely that her family would genuinely miss her.

Not her parents, especially.

Their sole purpose for having her there was to expose her as a failure and highlight the mess she had made of her life. However, her mother would have more ammunition to use against her when they next visited if she didn't show up. That in and of itself was motivation enough to keep going. Despite being used as the family's scapegoat, she never gave up on the idea that something would get better. She was going to find her own fairytale family, even if it meant pushing her parents every step of the way.

Unexpectedly, the automobile slipped, slamming into another patch of ice and startling Millie out of her reverie. She pressed the brake and attempted to avoid the fishtail that was almost yanking the wheel out of her hands.

The front of the car landed in a snow-filled ditch as she overcompensated and went off the road to the right.

She yelled, "Shit!" as she slammed her gloved hand down on the steering wheel. She climbed out and plunged half a foot into the snow, allowing the dampness to seep through her trousers and into her calves. Because she had assumed she would spend the entire time in her car, she had not bothered to wear snow boots. She now chastised herself for not having been more organized.

She turned to face the car and noticed that the driver's side rear wheel had completely lifted off the ground, causing the vehicle to sit unevenly in the slope. Knowing that she wouldn't be able to get it out on her own, she sighed. She reached into her jacket to find her phone, pulled off her glove, and made a call to her mother.

She knew that her mother would not be pleased when she called or begged for assistance on Christmas Eve, but she was at a loss for what to do. Millie could already hear her mother advising her to work through this situation on her own, but who else could she call? There was no sound from the phone. She was frustrated for a few seconds before realizing her call had not been received and she had no service.

After spending only a few minutes outside, Millie sank back into the hard, cold, leather. The car was still running, but there was no use in keeping the heat on when it was barely working. The storm persisted, but she was aware that she would have to venture outside to look for assistance or, at the very least, a secure location to wait it out. She would freeze by the time a car drove by if she stayed here. Furthermore, the outside temperature wasn't all that lower than it was inside the car. At least getting someplace would be warmer.

Someone had to live around here. From her past travels, she was aware that there were a few houses strewn among the trees, visible from the road when visibility wasn't completely obscured by a driving snowfall.

She reluctantly opened the driver's side door. She grabbed her purse from the passenger seat, slammed the door, and locked it, confident that nothing valuable would be found inside even if someone were to stumble upon it.

In order to at least have some support under her feet as she trudged through the snow, she climbed up onto the road. She struggled to maintain her balance as her tennis shoes seemed like they would slip on the ice. Pulling her scarf up to cover her ears, she nestled inside her coat. Her eyes burned as the ice cut at them. Though she could hardly see through the conditions that had undoubtedly developed into a snowstorm, she persisted. She had to take cover.

She squinted as she tried to see through the snow-covered veil, hoping to get a glimpse of something like distant lights, fireplace smoke, or the odd color of a passing car. After battling the wind and the cold, she may have just traveled a half mile, but her entire body ached as if she'd walked for ten, exhausted from the short journey. She was beginning to worry that she would lose a few toes. At this point, she'd vowed that if she came across an empty house, she wouldn't think twice about breaking in. Let them arrest her. At least a jail cell would be warm.

Millie was no longer genuinely aware of the ground under her, thus her feet merely moved against her will. She lost her balance and fell onto her hands, allowing the snow to seep through her flimsy gloves. Pushing up, she noticed a glimmer of optimism as she regained her footing.

She could just make out the outline of a massive cabin through the snow and wind-blown driveway. Millie rushed towards it, skidding on the ice like a deer with fresh legs.

When she finally made it to the door, a wave of relief passed through her. She firmly grasped the sturdy knocker and used her tense fingers to lift and drop it. She heard someone approaching and waited nervously. The door creaked open after another long moment. She was quickly comforted by a gust of warm, slightly smokey fireplace air, even with the storm behind her. But her mouth felt open as she realized who was there in front of her.

He was the one.

Millie

MILLIE NEVER WOULD HAVE THOUGHT that she would be seeing the scandal-tainted playboy in person. The one who she had been listening to on the radio only a short while before he was standing in front of her. In the absence of his usual silk tie and fancy suit, she almost couldn't recognize the man. His brown hair appeared dishevelled, as though he hadn't bothered to brush it after getting out of the shower. He was taller than she'd imagined he'd be, and the thin grey tee showed off an impressive set of shoulders. He had a sun-burnished glow about him that made him look as though he'd just returned from somewhere exotic, which, Millie was sure, wasn't unlikely. She thought she recalled seeing a grainy photo of him in a swimsuit and a woman in not much of anything on the cover of a tabloid when she was grocery shopping a few weeks back.

Naturally, witnessing him in person brought to light certain aspects that a camera could never portray, such as the intensity with which his dark eyes glowed when they were directly gazing at you and his lips curving into a frown. For someone who was barefoot and wearing plaid pajama pants, he had a rather intimidating appearance.

"Yes?" he inquired, projecting suspicion.

His question took her by surprise.

She had assumed that when the door was opened and her host saw her standing there, shivering and on the verge of death, she would be sufficiently alarmed to react. Nobody with a shred of empathy would, surely, abandon someone on a night such as this one. Naturally, though, she hadn't anticipated Hayden Dickinson to be the one to open the door. Considering the number of photographers that trailed him around, he was probably always on the lookout for people he didn't know well.

She could see his point of view because the press had not always been supportive, but she also knew that if she didn't get inside before frostbite set in, she wouldn't have another hand. There was a legitimate suspicion, and then there was the simple inability to act humanely. Millie watched to see where he would fall on the spectrum. She briefly thought about walking away and simply finding somewhere else, but she realized it was too late. She would never reach the next residence. Still, the cold burned like needles through her skin, and all she could manage was a look of bewilderment and a little moan. She was certain that her blood was freezing as she stood there.

"May I assist you?" he asked, clearly annoyed by her silence.

That's right, it's a failure to be human.

Even though she knew it was her best option, she didn't enjoy the idea of spending even a short time with this man as she waited for a tow truck—even though it would be just an hour or two. With a sigh, she swallowed her pride and accepted her fate.

For a little while, she could make herself be lovely. All she could hope was that he would follow suit.

"I...," her teeth chattered as she added, "I apologize for bothering you. But my car broke down and I need to call someone, but my phone doesn't have any service. Would it be okay if I used your phone?"

He just looked at her, obviously unsure whether to trust her enough to let her in and seemed irritated by her presence.

A pledge sealed in blood saying that she wasn't a tabloid

journalist—was that what he needed? If that's what he was going for, then tough luck for him. Her hands were too frigid to wield a pen, and her blood was too frozen to be useful.

She considered saying just that. However, she had enough experience biting her tongue and acting politely when she didn't want to be around her family.

Now she could use all that training.

"Please. I simply must make a phone call. As soon as the tow truck arrives, I will depart." Even though it was unbearable for her to say, she managed to stammer out one more, "Please," before waiting for his answer.

A dapper black lab approached the ajar door, waving its tail, and snuggled up against Hayden.

Millie wanted to dig her icy fingers into the dog's coat.

After bending over to pick up the dog's collar, Hayden peered out the door to survey the surroundings.

Was he thinking of letting me go back out into that?

She hoped he wouldn't, but all she could do was wait and see what he would decide. She thought he had forgotten she was in front of him, about to freeze to death, because he stared out into the darkness for so long. He withdrew just as she was certain he was about to send her on her way.

Would he slam the door in my face?

But no, all he did was sigh with annoyance and gesture inside.

"Fine," he answered in angry annoyance. "Won't you please come in?"

Her mouth fell open, and amazement momentarily immobilized her as his expression softened into irritation.

"Would you please hurry up? It's not too hot outside."

That jolted her out of her reverie and hurried through the doorway into the cozy, warm room. She wanted to cry because it felt so nice, and she stayed there for a while, savoring the heat emanating from the enormous hearth. She was eventually able to realize that she wasn't going to freeze to death after a few seconds, and her curiosity caused her to look around and truly take in her surroundings. Then her mouth fell open once more.

Hayden Carter's cabin in the woods was anything but rustic. The space had the appearance of an opulent ski lodge, from the enormous antler chandelier to the lofty vaulted ceiling fully covered in evergreens and a fireplace large enough to stand inside.

At last, Millie realized that Hayden was waiting for her to give her jacket to him by holding out his hand.

Well at least he can be a gentleman when he wants to be. More like he just didn't want me to ruin his floor with her snow dripping off of her.

That did seem like a better option. She took it off her shoulders and gave it to him, complete with her knitted scarf.

"Thank you. I'll be right back. What happened to your phone?"

She was still thawing out, despite her best efforts to sound confident, and she realized that the walk in the snow had worn her out.

"It's old, broken, and useless."

As she followed him into his kitchen, he pointed at a landline phone hidden in a pantry.

"Maybe it's best that I never got rid of this relic because my mobile is out too. However, I wouldn't put too much stock in the line holding up during this storm."

She said, "Do... um... do you have the yellow pages, by any chance?" She didn't know who to call for a tow, and it didn't seem like her phone could help her find the nearest service station.

She was surprised and relieved when he pulled out a phone book from a cabinet. "I guess it's a good thing I kept this on hand, but I never thought it would get used for anything other than kindling for the fireplace." With a laugh, he took a drink out of the refrigerator and left the room, his dog following close behind, leaving her all alone in the shadowy space.

She relaxed and took in her surroundings, feeling a little more at ease without his close presence. The cabin's facade had given it a modest appearance, but the more she saw, the more evident it was that the layout was intended to mimic architecture, concealing the fact that it was a playboy's hideout from onlookers. Massive windows surrounded the kitchen, offering what Millie could only imagine was an award-winning vista during non-whiteout conditions. She found it hard to believe that Hayden had ever been in the room other than to get drinks from the refrigerator because it looked as sterile and austere as a restaurant kitchen. Although there was clearly space for employees, he appeared to be the only person in the cabin with the dog. If not, he most likely would have dispatched a different person to handle the miscreants who appeared on his front porch.

Millie gave a shrug. It didn't matter because her goal was to flee as soon as possible.

Hayden

THE RELENTLESS HOWL of the wind echoed through the desolate night, swirling the snowflakes into a chaotic dance outside my cabin. The world beyond my door was an unforgiving canvas of white, a blizzard that seemed to have taken a personal vendetta against anyone daring to venture into its icy clutches.

Her hat, a feeble shield against the biting cold, clung to her head as if trying desperately to escape. The jacket that enveloped her seemed more like a makeshift survival suit than a fashion statement, and her jeans bore the unmistakable marks of a losing battle against the relentless snow. Wind-chapped cheeks and frozen strands of hair framed her face, giving her the appearance of someone who had just emerged victorious from a battle against nature itself.

There is something about her that made me open this door. After the attempt on my life, I was stupid for opening the door, but she seems so innocent, and small.

Joel and Mark, my stoic guardians, were absent—names replaced by roles, just as the replacements had stepped into their shoes. There was a void in security, an unsettling realization that the fortress I had built was momentarily vulnerable. Still, a sense of duty prevailed, an unspoken pact with my own humanity that forbade me from leaving someone to the mercy of the storm.

I was taught better than that.

So, I reluctantly allowed the woman entry. The promise lingered in the air—she could stay until rescue arrived, but not one moment more. I didn't want company longer than what was needed.

Damn women always want to be here, but she doesn't seem like other women at all.

As her emerald eyes met mine, a tingle ran through me, something I couldn't explain. She seemed to be so fragile and vulnerable, yet strong and resilient.

As she made the call, a strained conversation with a towing service, I observed from a distance. The desperation in her voice with the plea for assistance resonated in the quiet room. Her words painted a picture of urgency, of a desire to escape the frigid night and find solace within the warmth of family.

Yet, there lingered a peculiar note in her final words—a subtle dissonance, an incongruity that I couldn't quite pinpoint. It was a discordant melody, out of tune with the harmony of her plight. I listened intently, Tyler, my loyal companion, by my side.

The frustration in her sigh, audible even from a distance, told me that the call didn't go as planned. As the call concluded, the room fell into a tense silence. The decision to face the cold once more hung in the air.

Tyler, sensing the impending departure, thumped his tail in a rhythmic cadence. The woman moved towards the door, each step a deliberate act of determination. The layers of clothing returned, a shield against the relentless elements.

This woman… something about her makes me feel as if she will be the death of me.

Millie

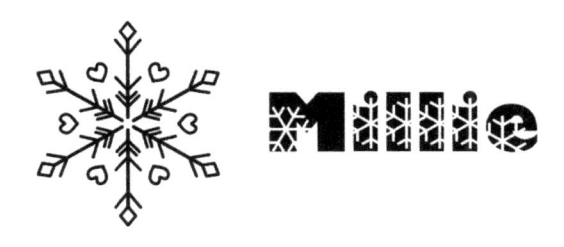

I'M NOT sure which would be worse—freezing to death or remaining at the cabin and having to put up with Hayden Dickinson's presence. Even though they would both be slow and agonizing, if I stayed, my chances of survival would be higher. I hoped that was the case. I turned slowly to look at him, trying to read something on his attractive poker face that appeared to be studying me.

Assessing me.

I was hungry and hadn't warmed up completely, but I didn't want to be evaluated by the powerful tabloid star. I shivered uncontrollably at the prospect of returning outside into the cold.

Maybe he'll let me wait inside, even though I don't want to be here.

I stood in front of him, getting more uneasy as he just stared at me. His gaze almost felt as if it was demanding me to talk.

Something about that look he's giving me is getting my intuition.

At last, I discovered my voice. "The tow truck company doesn't know when they can make it here. Is it okay if I call my family?" Uncomfortable, I pressed my hands together.

"Go ahead. I guess you can spend the evening at my house." He casually waved me back in the direction of the kitchen.

I fought the impulse to swoon over his adorable puppy as he lowered his head to rest on Hayden's thigh.

I quickly walked back into the kitchen, relieved to get out of his eyesight. His level of focus was intense. The man's wealth of over a billion dollars was understandable, given that he likely intimidated all those who dared to negotiate with him. After grabbing the phone again, I sank into a chair.

I wonder where the chef is at? There is no way HAYDEN DICK-ERSON would be cooking his own meal! Perhaps it was a heat and serve meal prepared by the chef earlier?

It smelled nice, no matter when or how it had been produced. I was almost tempted to steal a nibble as my tummy complained. Besides, I can't steal his food. I know better than that, even if he was offering me a place for the night.

"Hello?"

"Mia?" It sounded like my sister had already had a drink of wine to deal with our parents, or maybe five drinks.

"Millie! Hey, where are you now?"

"I'm stuck in the snowstorm. Could you please inform Mom and Dad that I won't be there tonight?"

She paused for a bit before saying, "Well, I think they thought you were here already."

That no one had really noticed her absence shocked Millie, but barely. As she responded, she rolled her eyes. "My car ran off the road on Route 4 because I got caught in the blizzard."

"Oh my God! Are you alright?"

At least someone loves me in the family. If I had told my parents, they would just criticize her for driving badly, not planning ahead, and who knows what else.

That's always the way it is.

"My car is stranded in a ditch, but I'm okay. I have to wait until morning because even though I called for a tow truck, they won't send anyone out in this storm. So I'm stuck here."

Her mother's faint, hardly discernible voice asked who was on the phone in the background. Millie winced as Mia responded, ready for the barrage of obscenities to start.

Snowed in with the Billionaire

Millie heard her mother yell, followed by a spiteful laugh. "That girl can't do anything right, so no surprise there." Millie's mother was interrupted by Mia, but she had already heard enough to make her eyes water.

I tried not to cry, biting my lip. She was aware that her work wasn't the most reputable or well-paying, but she did it because it was what she liked to do, and all she wanted was for her parents to be more encouraging. She said earnestly, "Just please let them know that I'll be there tomorrow."

"Avoid letting her affect you. You know how she is."

Millie remained silent.

"Well, then, I'm consuming all of your eggnog!" Mia exclaimed in a carefree manner.

I laughed at that. "It's alright, Mia. Please, just let them know."

"All right, don't stress over it. I will tell them." After a little pause, she said, "I truly appreciate that you phoned so I could warn you. I'm not sure it's a very good surprise, but Mom has one for you."

"What are you trying to say? How unexpected is that?"

"She kind of invited someone, I guess." My sister was forced to continue as I remained silent. "She extended an invitation to Matt."

"What?" I let out a cry into the phone, reducing my volume to keep Hayden from hearing. "How could she... why would she?" Not because she didn't want Matt to be present, but rather because she didn't want her mother to become involved and try to get Matt back for her.

"I apologize. I would have warned you about it sooner, but I didn't learn about it until this morning."

"It's alright. I suppose it's fortunate that I have the rest of the evening to prepare my response for him when I get there." Although there wasn't much to be happy about, something positive was present. She would have plenty of time to devise her strategy.

"So, where should I let them know that you're at?"

I was at a loss for words. She was unable to assert that she was with Hayden Dickinson alone. In any case, she wasn't positive if her sister would accept her story. "I walked to a home near where my car got stuck."

"A home? Like, at someone else's home?"

I grinned.

Not that Hayden Dickinson was a stranger. Everyone knew him.

"Don't worry, I'm all right." She dropped her voice and paused. "What a gentleman he is."

"Wait, a he? Is he attractive?"

"What are you going on about?" I had to try to keep my sister in the dark or face an endless amount of grilling.

"If you got stuck at a hot guy's house on Christmas Eve, it would be exactly like in the movies, right? Tell me, please. You will have cocktails with a hottie while lounging on a bearskin rug in front of the fireplace!"

I hesitated before answering. She was a terrible liar, and her sister would know it right away if she claimed the person she was spending the night with wasn't attractive. Furthermore, she didn't believe that Hayden Dickinson was keeping a low profile in this remote cabin because he wanted everyone to know where he was. She wasn't going to expose him if he was interested in keeping a low profile. Even though he might not be the kindest person, he was actually providing her with safety from the storm. She didn't want her presence to cause him any problems.

"Bearskin is disgusting," she murmured, sidestepping the inquiry. "Listen, all I'm doing this evening is making sure I get a good night's sleep so I can tackle the tow truck first thing tomorrow morning. I apologize for letting you down." I glanced around the corner to make sure Hayden hadn't heard me because she realized she was speaking louder than she had meant to.

"Please, I can tell he's hot by your voice. Before you head

home, go get some. If you know what I mean. Perhaps it will truly assist you in moving past Matt."

Even though she knew she would never be able to move on from him, she couldn't help but smile at that. Before hanging up, she told her sister how much she loved her.

Although she wasn't too excited to see Hayden in the living room, she needed to know the exact restrictions on her stay in his home because she was technically his guest. Since she didn't want to be here in the first place, she had no intention of going above and above in her welcome.

Rushing out of the kitchen, she almost bumped into him while he was finishing up his beer. Millie reddened, praying he hadn't overheard what she had said.

"Once more, thank you. I mean, for allowing me to use the phone."

He gave her a quick look, and she looked away.

God, what is it about him that makes me squirm?

His statement, "It's just a phone," made her feel foolish.

She observed him approach the cabinet adjacent to the stove, take out two plates, and set them down on the counter there.

"You must be starving." He phrased it as though she had no option but to respond in the affirmative. That tone, the one that said he knew he was a gift to womankind, was back. She wanted to refuse out of contrarian, but the truth was that she was ravenous, and whatever was being prepared smelt delicious and garlicky.

She tempered, saying, "I wouldn't want to put you in any trouble."

He sighed loudly, exasperated. "Please, would you just eat? I made entirely too much and I detest leftovers."

"You made that?" I was too shocked to disguise it. "What's it?"

"Alfredo feta. Among the numerous things I discovered during my year in Italy was this."

He had to humble-brag, of course.

With a serving spoon hanging above the pan, he turned to face her. It was difficult to recall words when his eyes met hers.

Was his attractiveness truly so distracting?

In a way, it felt unfair.

"You'll have some then?" Hayden queried.

She swallowed hard and nodded.

The dog approached Millie as he wriggled his way into the kitchen. It was good to have something to think about besides Hayden. "What is his name? Or her name?"

"His name is Tyler. The world's greatest dog."

He was never photographed with his dog by the press—she realized as she stroked the smooth fur of the puppy. There was an aspect of him that she was unaware of, yet there it was—snuffling her sneakers and giving her a playful tail wag.

"Do you want to top your pasta with extra parmesan cheese?" Hayden enquired as he opened the fridge. "Or is that going to be too much for your daily caloric intake?"

Millie got to her feet. "Pardon me? What do you mean by that?"

He cast a scowl her way. "Nothing. It's an easy question."

"You think I'm overweight?" Millie screamed at him.

"I didn't say that," Hayden stammered. "I am aware that the majority of the women I dine with have really stringent dietary needs. You have to walk the runway in underwear every day, so it kind of goes with the job. However, you obviously aren't a model."

I didn't believe the man could insult me any further, but somehow, he did. She gave him a fierce look and remained silent, not believing in her ability to control her tongue and say something hurtful to the man who was saving her from a snowstorm.

Hayden set a plate of pasta in front of her, seemingly oblivious to the effect of what he had spoken. Muttering, "Thank you." She bit into it, half-expecting it to be glue-like.

When the creamy, perfectly cooked spaghetti first touched her tongue, she suppressed a small groan.

Millie felt uneasy in the quiet and tried to think of something to say. She was certain that it was a delicate topic and that she probably shouldn't have asked, but she was at a loss on how to control her curiosity. Made the decision to extract some rumors from him so that, when she did go home, she could tell Mia all the information.

With her lips full, she questioned, "Were you hurt?"

He raised his head and met hers. "What are you talking about?"

"When you were shot today. Did you feel it? Did anything hurt you?"

"Do I appear injured?"

"Alright, not at all. Simply said, I mean... was it nearby? Do you know who fired a shot at you?" She had an instant regret for saying anything.

He shook his head and laughed a little. "No, and they failed horribly at it. I'm not sure who believed they would be competent enough to pull something like that off."

"So, are you just staying here until the shooter is located? Or are you here crying about it?"

"Crying? How on earth do you believe that I'm hiding? Nothing and no one exists that I would be running from." He pointed around the space. "One of my houses is this one. When I need some alone time, I come here."

She interpreted his cutting his eyes off at her as his way of ending the conversation.

She blushed and turned to gaze at the food on her plate. Regardless of what he said, there was no way he could have created the Alfredo, it was that delicious.

Perhaps the blonde who accompanied him to the gala was present and had taken care of the cooking? Perhaps she had prepared him dinner before going upstairs, and she was in the shower or already in bed? However, that seemed odd. Why prepare a special meal for two only to disappear before enjoying it?

"This tastes really good," she nudged. She wasn't concerned if the blond woman was still around, but she didn't want to be taken aback if she happened to stroll in and see Millie here.

Without bothering to glance up at her, he muttered, "Thanks."

"So, did you actually make this, or did your personal chef come in for a quick cookout so you could claim the credit?" Though she didn't try to come across as antagonistic, his icy demeanour was beginning to grow on her.

With a non-amused expression on his lips, he let go of his fork and reclined in his chair. "Do you really think I told lies?"

She parted her lips in response, then snapped it shut. If she angered him, he might decide to kick her out in the cold after all. "I just, well, I thought, I guess I figured you wouldn't have time to cook."

He raised his eyebrows inquisitively, so she continued, "I mean, you're a busy man, are you not? I only assumed that you wouldn't have the time. And you have the money to, well, to hire someone to do it for you. Right?"

"So, you assume that I don't cook? Or that I don't know how to cook?"

Millie fumbled over her words, and Hayden stopped her before she could get anything out. "It's rude to assume that you know someone based on the gossip about them." He paused. "I just realized that I don't even know your name."

"Millie," she softly answered. "Millie Jeremy."

"Okay, Ms. Jeremy. Well, in my opinion, it's inappropriate to make assumptions about a person you don't know. I happen to enjoy cooking in my free time and have never had a chef on my personal staff, with the exception of when one is needed for an occasional banquet or party. Contrary to what you might believe, I happen to be a very self-sufficient individual."

Millie bristled. Yes, he was her host, and yes, she was dependent on his generosity for a place to stay tonight—but she didn't appreciate being condescended to. She got enough of that from her family. She wasn't about to put up with it from a spoiled billionaire.

"I appreciate your little lesson here, Mr. Dickinson, but I'm sure you've made your own assumptions about me, have you not? As for not knowing you, you've made a great deal of yourself and your personal life public knowledge. It's rather difficult to not know you. When you put your life on the front page, can you blame people for drawing conclusions?"

"Oh really? Well, Ms. Jeremy, what is it that you know of me, then?" He crossed one ankle over the opposite knee and looked at her like she was the next course.

Millie hadn't expected to have to explain herself and was caught off guard by the request. She looked away, flustered by his unwavering gaze. She wracked her mind for something she really knew… and was embarrassed to realize that most of her knowledge of him was based on gossip, suggestion, and innuendo. Some of it was probably true—but she couldn't say for sure what those things might be—and if she guessed and got it wrong, it would just give him another excuse to laugh at her. Better to back down. "I'm sorry, I just… never mind."

She could feel his eyes on her, and after several uncomfortable moments, she finally met his gaze.

He had one eyebrow cocked upwards; his mouth turned down in a frown. "Do yourself a favor and keep your thoughts to yourself from here on. I won't claim to be the most generous of hosts, but I promise that I'm far more generous than that storm will be to you." He motioned his head towards the front door before sliding out from the table, snatching up both plates and tossing them into the sink.

Hayden

He had no idea that he would end up with a spitfire on his hands when he opened the door to this woman, Millie Jeremy. She had appeared to be a kitten who was left outside in the storm. He wasn't used to people being so eager to provoke him, and it appeared like that was all she was doing at the moment.

Why did I even answer the door?

He was eager for the morning to arrive because he would finally be done with her. He might be able to survive the night. Anyhow, it was almost time for bed.

The day had been exhausting and lengthy. He was worn out.

Damn my life. Why do I even do what I do anymore? I should just quit.

He was so exhausted that his judgment was clouded. That must be why he found himself wondering exactly how far down that blush could go and thinking she looked exceptionally pretty when she blushed.

The thought caused Hayden to hesitate, feeling a stirring beneath his belt.

Boy, get down.

That response—what the hell was that? For heaven's sake, he'd slept with supermodels. How could a scruffy little snow creature like that draw a rise out of him?

He gave a headshake. The only possible reason was that

he was just horny, there was no other option. Sure, she was attractive but not what he was used to being with. Obviously not his style, but not awful either.

Not at all awful.

He had the best view of her behind as she leaned over to pet Tyler. A small part of him wanted to walk right up to her and give it a good slap.

"Pardon me!"

When Hayden realized she had seen him watching, he jerked up his eyes. Naturally, she was frowning, but had her blush become a little more intense?

As usual, he skilfully sidestepped the topic by clearing his throat and crossing his arms. "I've just realized that the sleeping arrangements aren't going to work."

She appeared doubtful. "In this location? You must have 10 bedrooms up there, I wager." Millie gestured to the shining stairway made of blonde wood over her shoulder.

He stated calmly, "If you bet that, then you'd lose. I use a room for my office and a room for my gym; those are the only rooms upstairs, along with the master suite."

He sighed in exasperation, and she scowled as though she didn't believe him.

"I come here when I want to be alone, as in by myself, like I mentioned to you. I don't bring visitors here, so why am I prepared to receive them? I believe you'll be more comfortable down here on the couch, but if you're dead bent on sleeping upstairs, feel free to curl up on my weight bench."

Millie glanced beyond him to the couch covered in burgundy velvet. "You refer to the item? Given that it's as large as a king bed, I should feel at ease."

"Well, that's resolved," he said, advancing to the enormous storage box that served as both a coffee table and a storage area.

On one of his business excursions to Paris, he came upon the item—a historic steamer trunk—that cost as much to bring home as it had to buy it. Hayden quickly cleared the platter and the pricey glass trinkets his designer insisted he use to set it up before he opened it.

He took out two thick cream-colored blankets that were furry to the touch, and he set them onto the couch. "This should keep you warm enough." From the corner of his eye, he witnessed her startle.

"I'm grateful."

"No worries," he stated firmly. "Tyler likes to sleep in front of the fire sometimes, so I'll make sure to keep him away."

"You don't have to," Millie retorted. "His presence would be appreciated."

With a snap of his head, Hayden looked at her.

"If you need a shower, use the upstairs bathroom. If not, there's a powder room just by the front door. It's the first door on the left when you ascend to the landing."

For a brief moment, the idea of her taking off her clothes for a shower distracted him, but he quickly got over it.

"I'll be alright," she replied, giving Tyler another pet. "I appreciate your hospitality,"

She just wouldn't give up, damn it.

"Alright, good night." Whistling for Tyler, he turned to go.

He was stopped in his tracks as she remarked, "Sorry, one more thing."

He gently turned to face her.

Is there anything more the woman could ask for?

"Please could I have a pillow?"

He nodded curtly to her. "Give me a minute."

For him to be taking care of her felt so strange. He wasn't used to having requests made of him when there were employees available to handle them. However, there was no staff present. He had sent them all away since he'd wanted to be alone, but instead, a woman had turned up on his doorstep, stranded.

With Tyler walking behind him, he marched up the stairs

and into the master suite, snatching a pillow off his enormous bed before stomping back down to the big room.

He noticed she looked... different as he moved closer to her.

Her hair fell beyond her shoulders, framing her face and falling halfway down her back in rich, reddish-brown waves. She had taken off the baggy sweater and had a tucked basic black t-shirt underneath, hugging her petite but strong figure. Her face glowed in the firelight, and her jade green eyes were framed by the flames that reflected in the tiny wire-frame glasses that now rested over the bridge of her nose.

He took a quick look down her body and scolded himself for it. He didn't need to be lusting for a woman who obviously detested him; he already had enough troubles in life.

Approaching silently, he handed her the pillow, before turning to leave her alone.

She stopped him with a hand on his arm as he turned sharply. With a tip of her chin, she stated, "Thank you. And have a nice evening."

"Good night."

He stalked over to the staircase, eager to leave her alone.

"Mr. Dickinson?"

Damn it woman! Just let me get this fucking day over with will you?

He reluctantly turned to look at her.

"I know this is an inconvenience for you, but is it really necessary to treat me so rudely?"

He was done.

"And do you really have to treat me like this with everything you say and every wrong belief you hold, Ms. Jeremy? Even when you're forced to acknowledge that you don't really know anything about me, you still choose to believe the worst about me. You are in my house, you've eaten my food, and you will be sleeping under my roof—safe and warm—rather than being stranded outdoors and freezing to death in the cold, even though I may not be the best host."

He slammed his fist on the railing post.

"Are you truly under the impression that the appropriate way to act as a guest is to sneer at me and accuse me of not being as kind as you seem to believe you deserve? Not feeling like I could handle being around other people after someone tried to kill me, which is why I'm here, to be ALONE. Feel free to believe that I'm some sort of ogre. But as you stand there enjoying the fruits of my hospitality, such as it is, I'll be grateful that you didn't chastise me like a naughty child. I think I've been more than accommodating, so please don't ask for things from me that I'm not obligated to provide."

He turned and took one step up.

Her voice stopped him again. "I am aware that you are not obliged to do anything. I simply... all I can say is that it would make our time together a little bit more enjoyable if you did more than merely accept me being here." She took a minute to allow her words to register with Hayden.

"You and I are not buddies, Ms. Jeremy. I know you're only here for a little while, but if you don't like how you've been treated, feel free to risk it with the storm. But if you want to benefit from the kindness that I have extended to you, then early in the morning, when my..." He hesitated, trying to think of the word. Although, in a sense, they were bodyguards, he didn't want to refer to them as such. They were definitely not buddies; thus, he was unable to call them that. He would not trick himself into thinking they were interested in anything but their income. "My associates will help you get back on the road when they return, so you won't have to worry about my bad manners anymore. Until then, have a good night."

He quickly stomped up the stairs, making it into his bedroom, slamming the door, and instantly regretted it. It betrayed his emotional state, something he tried hard to keep hidden from people he didn't trust, not because it could have frightened the domineering intruder currently dozing on his pillow. He wasn't used to needing to be on guard up here, but damn it. This house served as his haven, his escape from the outside world. It may not have been as large as his estate or as ostentatious as his penthouse flats, but it exuded a coziness and security that he had never fully discovered elsewhere.

Tonight, that emotion didn't appear to exist.

Though, not because of what had occurred that day at the gala. No, this was all due to the damn woman in his house, sleeping on his couch, annoying him with every breath she took.

He quickly undressed and then got into bed.

The fire blazed from across the room, from when he started it before she got here, yet the covers felt cold against his skin. Before long, the room would grow warm, and the cool sheets would start to feel refreshing. He would shiver up until that point from the silk rubbing against his nude body. He pulled a pillow under his head and watched the dancing light on his ceiling after stretching and letting his muscles relax from the stress of the day.

He imagined the woman lying on his couch.

Was she fully dressed under those blankets?
Just in her underwear? What kind of underwear did she have on?
Was she naked just like me?

He tried to push the questions out of his mind, but it was too late. His cock was hard as steel as he thought of her.

What the fuck is it about this damn woman?

He didn't want any connections or commitments, it was why he didn't interact with women such as Millie. They were too challenging and demanding but god that was a turn on at the same time. That wasn't how his women were. His women were easy-going, agreeable, and content with whatever life had to offer during their brief time together.

He used them, and they used him.

So why, at that moment, was he as rigid as a bone because of Millie Jeremy? Why did his cock pulse thinking of her lying nude on his couch? Why did he want to snatch a handful of her hair, pull her head back, and crash his mouth on top of hers at the sight of her watching him over the rim of her glasses?

Damnit, I forgot to throw a fucking log into the fire downstairs. Fucking woman… god I want to fuck her… no I don't, stop it!

He could only imagine how cold the large room would grow as the night went on, what with flames going. Even though he didn't like having her around, he wasn't going to abandon her to shiver for the better part of the night.

Hayden jumped back out of bed, jerked his trousers back on as he willed his erection to deflate, and moaned instinctively.

After opening the door, he descended the stairs once more in the direction of the woman he had made up his mind not to want.

Millie

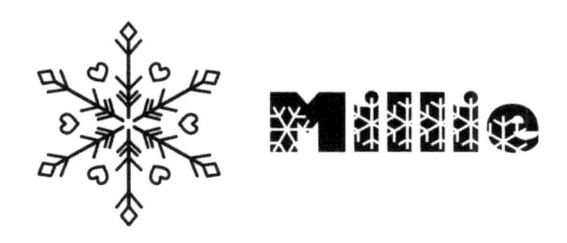

She woke up shivering and was even more grateful for the luxurious blankets that covered her as she listened to the wind howling around the house, making her feel a draft. She blinked her eyes tiredly, noticing it was dark in the room.

The fire must have gone out.

She burrows down into the blankets more trying to get warm as she throws her head back.

Was this place haunted, or was the noises she kept hearing just Hayden pacing above her in his room? She was eager for the night to end so she wouldn't have to stay under the arrogant bastard any longer. All she wanted was to return home to her family, to convince her parents that she wasn't a total failure, and to find a way to win Matt back. Then go home.

I've been rude to Hayden. I based my reactions on him from what I saw in the tabloids and that wasn't fair to him. BUT he was rude to me too. What is it about the man that infuriates me… and turns me on all at once?

Once more, she heard footsteps, but they were coming down the steps. Millie curled up beneath the cover. Maybe if she just pretended to be asleep, he would ignore her, as she didn't want to face him again, at least until she had to.

He stepped toward the couch and she felt him lean over its back, hovering just over her for a little while. Millie shivered as she clamped her eyes shut and willed her body to calm down.

"Do you feel cold?"

His voice stunned Millie, making her jump. He was standing there, peering down at her with a piercing glare, when she opened her eyes.

Without a shirt.

Damn the man!

With a forceful swallow, she moved the blanket closer to her chin.

"If you would like, I could light the fire again." It was just a statement rather than a question.

He had already moved to the fireplace, throwing in two logs, and stood waiting, staring at her.

"No, thank you; I'm fine," she instinctively objected.

"You're shivering, it's freezing down here. I'll leave you to return to sleep quickly."

She didn't know how she'd fall back asleep. It took awhile the first time. An unusual Christmas, in a strange house with a strange man. No matter how comfortable and toasty he made it for her, she was not going to get any sleep. All she wanted was daylight to arrive so she could go, either in the company of Mr. Dickinson's "associates" or with the tow truck driver.

"Do you want to have another blanket?"

The fire had ignited behind him, and despite her glasses not being on her nose, she was still able to make out his broad shoulders, toned stomach, and strong chest. She didn't want to let her gaze linger, but even in the dark, she couldn't help it. Her nipples hardened as she imagined what she wanted to do to him.

She could almost feel her fingers traveling across his softly tanned skin, where her fingertips would run over his firm nipples. Then she would slowly drag her nails across his hips and beneath the elastic band of his plaid pajama pants.

Gah!

Stop it!

I will not allow you to invade my dreams and make me wish to share your damn bed!

Snowed in with the Billionaire

"Mr. Dickinson, what are you trying to say with all of this sudden care for me? What caused the shift in sentiment?"

He was sitting at the far end of the huge couch, as far away from her as he could manage, and she could see him straining to find the right words. She frowned.

"It's been a pretty exhausting day," he stated.

"So, I've heard," she muttered. And with that, she began to feel even more ashamed of her own actions. It couldn't have been nice to have a stranger enter his house at a time when he must have already been feeling vulnerable after going through something so awful.

A hush fell over both of them.

She didn't know what to say. She felt that she ought to apologize as well, but she was at a loss for words to say it.

Pulling the blanket up to her chin, she sat up, hugging it tight around her like a shield, shielding herself not from the cold but from him and the attraction she could not shake even though she knew it was a bad idea. The presence of him in the room suddenly made her feel quite uneasy. Beneath the layers, she was starting to perspire, but there was hardly any flame.

God, why didn't you put a shirt on before coming down here?

Regardless of his intentions, he was incredibly distracting. She sat stone cold still, waiting for him to say something, do something.

"Since I was a teenager, I have never shared this cabin with anyone before."

She couldn't decide if he was talking to her directly or more to himself. She remained quiet, letting the emptiness linger between them once more. The heat from the fire was now blazing throughout the room.

A few minutes later, Hayden spoke once more. "I prefer wood heat, so I keep the furnace on low." He hesitated a minute, but Millie remained silent. "Nothing compares to the warmth and glow of a fireplace, don't you think?"

She gave him a smile and cocked her head, but then she swiftly snapped her head back forward after noticing how his bare chest seemed to gleam in the firelight.

"Yes, I do concur. It reminds me of joyful moments, family, and loved ones." She paused, not intending for the last one to escape her lips. Even though there was no suggestion that she meant him, it felt strange that she should say anything like that in front of him. There was no doubting that he had been spotted with numerous different ladies, whether or not the stories surrounding him were accurate.

Authentic, enduring love didn't appear to be in his plans.

"Happy times," muttered the man to himself. "Yes, I understand that you have a lot of amazing memories to cling to and that you grew up in a very close, loving family."

Was he sounding a little... envious, or am I just imagining it?

She paused. Even though she was staying with him and using his couch for the night, she didn't know him well enough to confide in him about her unhappy upbringing. In addition, his success had come from his relentless ambition as a businessman. She doubted he had much time in his life to deal with more delicate feelings.

How could he possibly comprehend what she had gone through?
How it had wounded her?

He gave off the impression of being the kind to advise her to turn her hardships into opportunities to grow. Such suggestions disgusted her. She wasn't superhuman as a result of her hardships; rather, they had just accustomed her to hardship. Was there any power in that? Perhaps, but there was also vulnerability. She was so over the battle of having to prove herself to the people who were meant to love her without conditions. In strange ways, it left her vulnerable, made her more easily damaged.

She needed to change the direction of the conversation because she didn't want to get into any of that. He had not spent much of his childhood in the press. She knew little about his early years other than the fact that he was an only child. She found the notion itself weird. She was unable to envision growing up without her parents.

Was his better?

"How about your early years?" she inquired. "How did your parents raise you?"

Though she wasn't wearing her glasses, she could still feel his gaze on her, but she was unable to interpret his expression because of the darkness and blurriness. Now as she had reached for them, he had turned away once more, gazing into the flickering flames.

All of a sudden, Mr. Dickinson was a riddle that Millie really wanted to solve.

Hayden

HAYDEN JUST STARED into the fire, silent.

Why was she concerned?

What made her inquire about him and his family?

He had no intention of speaking to her or informing her of what he had left behind. His past was just that, the past, and it was unrelated to the present. It was unrelated to the kind of man he was.

They had nothing to do with who he was now, and he was glad he didn't follow what they wanted.

If his parents had had their way, he would be employed at a factory producing auto parts and spend his weekends with their two children and the kind of bride they expected him to have. Joanie, who would be six, and Nicholas, who would be nine, would most likely be their names. He would receive ten vacation days after working for the company for eight years. He would use these days to spend a week at Christmas with his family and a week in the summer with his wife's family, switching places the next year. Every month or so, he would take his half-rusted, ancient Toyota Camry into the repair, and his wife would drive a minivan to transport their kids and all of their friends from soccer practice to dancing lessons. His parents had desired for him to have that kind of life, to lead a modest, calm, and typical life, barely making ends meet. Their perfect life, but not his.

Given that these details had no bearing on the guy he was becoming in the present, there was no reason to discuss them with this stranger. No matter how much he might want her.

She exhaled into the silence, giving in to whatever inner struggle she was going through, and he could feel her eyes on him.

"Okay, let me speak first. Which is odd, because it's not something I like to talk about," she muttered. "Hey, but, to whom will you tell about me? It's not as though you are acquainted with my family or will even recall me when I'm gone. How about I tell you about mine? I'll simply say it out loud now. To put it mildly, my childhood was horrible."

He caught a glimpse of her out of the corner of his eye as she lowered her head to gaze at her hands resting on her lap. He remained quiet, offering the woman his unspoken encouragement to keep going.

"My father is a neurologist who is adamant that he is superman and that for someone to matter as a human, they must be at least as accomplished as he is. He was in the Marines for ten years, the last four of which he used to complete his bachelor's degree. My mother is an alcoholic who became a housewife and leeches off of my father's pay. She met him while working as a receptionist at the hospital where he interned at. Her philosophy on life is that a woman ought to marry into a wealthy family and then live it up. She has only succeeded in inventing every conceivable vodka concoction and single-handedly sustaining Advil's operations. My sister and I have been best friends for a long time because of the criticism we received from our parents. We bonded to get through our childhood. Dad would always give us lectures about how vital education was. We turned our house into a boot camp for military personnel to ensure we continued to receive straight A's. We were only permitted to devote our time to extracurricular activities if they helped advance our careers. And the only legitimate professions were those in law, medicine, or some similarly esteemed field. Dance, athletics, and the arts all of these were forbidden from our home since they were deemed to be a waste of time."

Millie let out a sigh as she fidgeted into a new position.

"Mom used to lecture us on how important it was to be attractive and sought after, even as small children. As our parents looked for a suitable match for each of us, we were literally pimped out to other well-to-do families with boys our age or a year or two older. Although our parents were very particular about who they wanted us to marry, our marriages weren't exactly planned." She hesitated, caught in a state of internal turmoil.

He was actually fascinated now. Her family appeared to be completely different from his in every aspect. A part of him wished his father had shared Millie's father's ambition.

When she refused to go on, Hayden asked, "What took place? Have you tied the knot?" The fact that he knew the answer to the question suddenly mattered a great deal, even if he hadn't planned on asking the next question. "Are you in a marriage?"

Hayden was moved to join in by Millie's wonderful, lyrical laugh, but he couldn't recall the last time he had actually felt the need to laugh at anything.

"Wed?" she cried out. "Oh my god, no!"

Hayden had to admit that he was snorting this time at her response. He would have responded pretty much the same way if the question had been directed at him. She gave a small huff. "I said they had expectations, not that I did as they wanted. I almost got married, to be honest. We selected a day and all the details."

Hayden wasn't sure whether she stopped because she still felt pain from thinking about this man or because she believed Hayden wasn't interested, but he was really fascinated. Fearing that she would shut down and decide she'd told enough, he was afraid to try to get more information out of her; but as they sat there in silence, he recognized that she probably had. Therefore, asking would not have hurt him. She would respond to the question, skirt it, or ignore him.

"Whatever happened to this man you were going to marry? Your parents must have been really upset when the wedding was called off."

Millie let out a sigh and turned to face him, her auburn waves cascading over one shoulder as the fire's light created deep shadows on her flawless face. With her back against the sofa arm, she was sitting just inches away from him with her feet spread wide. It was a very sensual action, but yet very casual. He would touch her if he just put his hand on the couch next to his thigh. Even though her lithe form was hidden from view by the cover, she was still quite close. He immediately readjusted his position to prevent the flames from casting a noticeable shadow across his stomach as soon as he felt that tightening in his crotch again.

"My parents were livid. In fact, because of that we didn't talk to each other for a whole year. I didn't even spend Christmas with them last year." In shame, she lowered her eyes. "My parents' residence is five hours' drive away from my apartment. I kept calling and leaving a ton of messages, but nobody picked up or returned my calls. I reasoned that they couldn't be so callous as to turn me away if I drove up and stood on their front steps."

He noticed that her eyes were wet and gleamed from the light that briefly captured her eyes before her tears started falling down her cheeks. He leaned forward, not realizing what he was doing until he did it, and wiped her tears off her cheeks. "But they did turn you away, right?"

She withdrew slightly, disguising the gesture with a head nod in response to his query. "The man my parents wanted me to marry decided he didn't want to be with me, so they turned me back out into the cold. All my life, I had believed that I would be the one to decline the marriage, that I would not be able to carry it through. But in the end, it was me that desired it and not him."

"But you're now on good terms with them?"

Millie laughed. "If that's what you want to call it. My sister, Mia, invited me to Christmas dinner over the phone a month ago. After months of trying to convince them to even acknowledge my existence, she had finally worn them down to the point where they consented to let me come to a family event. At the time, I couldn't quite believe her when she told me that my parents wanted me to be there. It's even more difficult for me to believe now."

She giggled quietly and shook her head. Her dark waves caught the fire and formed a halo as her hair swung behind her and detached from her shoulder. "My sister, who I spoke with earlier, acknowledged that my parents were unaware that I wasn't present. They didn't seem to care that I almost died while traveling through a storm to get to them. She also mentioned that my mom had invited another person. Matt, my ex-fiance, is the guest."

She lifted her eyes to meet his, and he was struck, as he stared at her incredulously, by how bright and pure they were. "But that's just my mother's nature. If when things don't go as planned and she has any influence over it, she takes it."

"So, tell me, Matt, what made him so amazing?"

She paused, parted her lips in response, and then slammed it closed again in an instant. "I apologize. I speak way too much. How about you? What Christmas plans do you have?"

His eyes squinted for a second, then he grinned broadly. "Are you not going to answer my question?" He waited for her response, cocking his head to the side. "Are you worried that I might take offense?"

Hayden laughed as she responded by biting her lip.

"Don't hold back now since you weren't too worried about upsetting me earlier. Tell me."

Though he wasn't sure why, he was curious as to why their relationship hadn't succeeded.

It doesn't really matter.

It's not like I'll be seeing her again after she leaves in the morning.

Millie

MILLIE'S HEART quickened as she felt a pang of worry as she discussed her life with Hayden.
Why am I telling him all of this?
Well, at least we'll never see each other again after this.
She remained sitting in the dimly lit living room of Hayden's house, staring at him in anticipation of a response. Anxiety made her sweat, the act of sharing what she'd never told anyone before making her nervous and scared. The silence hung heavy, making seconds feel like minutes.
I can't believe I overshared with him, he'll probably go running scared or kick me out tonight.
Hayden finally gave up, and she let out the breath that she hadn't realized she had been holding for so long. Suddenly he asked, "I understand that it's late, but would you like a coffee?"
Her eyes flickered to her phone, noting the lateness of the hour. The possibility of having more conversations with Hayden sparked a delightful warmth within her, despite the fact that sleep appeared to be elusive.
What the fuck is wrong with me?
What is it about this man?
"Yes, that does sound pleasant," she said.
Hayden nodded toward the hearth, a subtle agreement to keep their conversation discreet so as not to disturb Tyler, who rested comfortably in the corner. The flames that were flick-

ering cast shadows that were dancing on the walls, which was a reflection of the delicate ballet of emotions that was taking place between Millie and Hayden.

As they proceeded to the kitchen, Millie's fingers reflexively grabbed for Hayden's arm, a momentary touch that sent thrills through her. The unexpected intimacy left her cheeks heated and goosebumps following in its wake. She withdrew her hand swiftly, thinking he wouldn't notice the outward manifestation of her emotion.

"Let me," she whispered, her voice a hesitant symphony in the quiet room.

Hayden nodded, studying her with an oddly gracious look on his face. Millie's earlier experiences at The Hideout, a coffee shop, her abilities recognized by the owner, now came to her help as she sifted through Hayden's kitchen, gathering the ingredients for a coffee that would display her competence.

His surprise kindness surfaced again as he inquired, "Do you need any help?" Standing near enough for her to feel the warmth of his presence, he collected two cups, his breath whispering against her neck.

A smile filled her lips as she worked. "No, I'm grateful. This is my work, in a way." The rhythmic sounds of grinding beans filled the air as she concentrated on the task at hand.

The talk went toward flavoured syrups, a world where Hayden revealed his preference for chocolate over coffee. Millie's laughter reverberated through the kitchen as she understood the absurdity of a self-proclaimed coffee expert refraining from the very beverage he claimed mastery over.

As the coffee took shape, banter flowed, and a companionship blossomed. The warmth in the room spread beyond the blazing fire, wrapping around them like a loving embrace. Millie marvelled at the unexpected turn of events, recognizing that, according to her assumptions, she wasn't as miserable as she had feared.

Snowed in with the Billionaire

Returning to the couch with their concoctions, they snuggled in, the fire throwing a fascinating glow. Hayden, in a rare moment of sensitivity, explained the history of the house, its significance, and the seclusion he had become accustomed to. Millie couldn't help but worry about the unseen portions of his life, sensing that there was more beneath the surface.

"I haven't had anyone stay in this house with me since I was a teenager, would you believe that?" Hayden said.

The tenderness in his words tugged at her heartstrings.

"It was my grandfather's childhood house, handed down to me."

Millie's curiosity got the better of her. "Why not? It's a stunning location. If you don't like it, why not sell it? Or do you think you'd live here with a wife in the future?"

A cloud went over Hayden's gaze, and his response was buried in uncertainty. "Maybe someday. But nobody has... attracted my attention up until now."

Millie chose not to press further, recognizing the barriers Hayden had constructed around his history. The peaceful understanding between them developed, and she found herself appreciating the shared vulnerability.

"So, what do you do out here if this is your private place?" she inquired, seeking to break the weight that lingered in the air. "Simply sit in silence? When you live your entire life in the headlines, doesn't that seem strange?"

Hayden's stare had a glimmer of contemplation as he contemplated her question, as if he were peeling back the layers of a long-kept truth. "Living in the headlines, as you put it, makes solitude a rare gift. Sometimes, the quiet moments become a refuge, a haven away from the relentless scrutiny. It's a paradox, really."

Millie listened, sensing the weight underlying his words. She was amazed at the complexities of a life lived in the public glare and the seclusion hidden beneath the grandeur of Hayden's lifestyle.

The fire crackled, throwing shadows that danced against the wall.

"Do you ever feel like you're missing out on something?" she questioned, her voice faint, a whisper borne by the night.

Hayden's eyes remained on the flames, his countenance a mix of concentration and melancholy. "There are moments when I wonder if the headlines have overshadowed the simple joys, the quiet happiness that eludes me in the limelight. But it's a choice, I suppose, a trade-off for the life I lead."

Millie nodded.

"I never expected the night to unfold like this," Hayden confessed, disturbing the serene silence. "It's been a long time since I've had such genuine conversation."

Millie smiled, her heart echoing the message. "Life has a way of surprising us, doesn't it? I'm grateful for this unexpected connection."

"Millie," Hayden began, his voice carrying a delicate doubt, "I've spent so much of my life in the public eye, surrounded by superficial connections. But tonight, it feels different. There's a genuine connection here, something I haven't experienced in a long time."

She met his stare, her pulse throbbing in tune with the unspoken feelings. The vulnerability in his comments connected with her own longing for sincerity. In that common understanding, Millie found the strength to articulate what had been lurking on the margins of her thoughts.

"I feel it too, Hayden. Tonight has been... unexpected, in the best possible way. Maybe there's something more here, something that goes beyond the headlines and the worlds we come from."

Hayden

As Millie twirled her cup of hot coffee, her eyes betrayed her vulnerability. The flickering light from the fire cast shadows that danced across her face, highlighting the traces of inner turmoil. She spoke, her words laced with a hint of melancholy, "Right now, you should be at home with your family, and I should be at home with mine."

She's right.

But I'm glad I'm here with her.

"Is it Matt, or is it your family, that you want to go home to?" Hayden's voice carried a subtle tremor, a touch of vulnerability that mirrored Millie's own.

She shook her head, her gaze fixed on the last of the coffee in her cup. "I haven't seen him in such a long time." The words lingered in the air, filled with the weight of unspoken history. Millie's eyes met Hayden's, revealing a storm of emotions within. "I'm just not sure," she admitted, her voice a fragile whisper.

As Millie contemplated her past, Hayden felt an unexpected surge of jealousy at the mention of Matt's name. The realization hit him like a wave, stirring emotions he hadn't anticipated. He wanted to understand the complexities of Millie's heart, to unravel the intricacies that made her who she was.

What the fuck did this Matt do to this amazing woman?

To make her so vulnerable and hurt.

Hayden pressed further. "Not much has changed in my opinion. What about Matt? Has he changed in any way since he concluded that you weren't what he wanted in the end?"

Millie's sigh echoed through the silence, a poignant acknowledgment of the passage of time. "It's only been a little over a year, so I doubt that much has changed to cause him to see things differently."

Hayden silently sipped his coffee, absorbing the intensity of the moment, hoping she'd continue to get everything off her chest.

Millie continued, her voice carrying the weight of unresolved emotions, "And what is expected of him seeing me? To reawaken emotions he once felt? No. He hasn't changed his mind, I'm sure of it."

Hayden placed his coffee mug on the table, his eyes never leaving Millie's. "But you won't know until you go home, will you?" he remarked, a note of understanding in his voice. "Despite him ending things, you still seem caught up on him. So, what makes him so wonderful?"

There better be something about him otherwise I'm going to go kick his ass.

Millie took a deep breath before responding.

Millie's eyes, now glistening with a mixture of vulnerability and resilience, met Hayden's gaze head-on. The flickering firelight played on her features, casting a soft glow that illuminated the turmoil within. "It's not about him being wonderful," she began, her voice a fragile melody. "It's about the memories we shared, the moments that once felt like they'd last forever."

Hayden leaned back, absorbing her words.

Millie continued, "We had dreams together, plans for the future. And when it all crumbled, those dreams didn't just disappear. They lingered, haunting the corners of my mind. I wanted them even though I knew I couldn't."

Snowed in with the Billionaire

Her fingers traced the rim of her cup, creating a soft percussion against the ceramic. "I've changed, Hayden. Life has changed. But those memories, they're like fragments of a beautiful disaster. I can't shake them off, no matter how much time has passed."

As Millie spoke, Hayden found himself drawn into the depths of her narrative. It was a tale of love, loss, and the persistent echoes of what once was.

"What if he hasn't changed?" Millie asked, her gaze piercing through Hayden's defences. "What if he hasn't had a change of heart? And what if I go back, only to find that the past is an unyielding anchor? Why did they invite him to dinner anyway?"

Hayden, grappling with his own insecurities and unspoken desires, met her gaze with a mixture of empathy and understanding. "Sometimes, Millie," he said, his voice a gentle murmur, "we find ourselves tethered to the past not because it defines us, but because we fear the unknown future. It's the uncertainty that keeps us anchored, not the person we once knew. I'm sure your parents invited him, hoping that you'd work things out and get back together again."

The silence that followed was pregnant with unspoken emotions.

Millie, her eyes shimmering with a newfound clarity, broke the stillness. "Maybe it's time to confront the unknown," she mused, her voice resonating with a quiet determination. "To unravel the mysteries of what lies ahead, even if it means leaving behind the fragments of the past."

Hayden nodded, a silent acknowledgment of the courage it took to embrace the uncertain.

Hayden, sensing the pivotal moment, leaned forward, his eyes locked onto Millie's. "The unknown can be daunting," he admitted, his voice carrying the weight of his own uncertainties. "But it's also where possibilities unfold. It's where we discover who we truly are, beyond the shadows of our past."

Millie, her gaze still fixed on him, absorbed his words. The warmth of the coffee cup in her hands contrasted with the cool uncertainty that enveloped her heart. "I've been holding onto what was," she confessed, her voice a delicate whisper. "But maybe it's time to release that grip and step into the uncertainty, even if it's frightening."

Hayden's eyes softened with understanding. "Fear is a part of every journey, Millie. It's the companion that whispers doubts in our ears. But sometimes, the most beautiful stories emerge from the willingness to face that fear, to confront the unknown with open hearts."

Millie took a deep breath, as if inhaling the courage to navigate the uncharted waters ahead. "I don't want to be defined by what's behind me," she said, her gaze flickering with newfound resolve. "I want to find out who I am now, and what the future holds."

Hayden nodded, a silent affirmation of her journey. "We're shaped by our experiences, but we're not confined by them," he remarked, his words resonating with a wisdom earned through his own battles. "The person you were with him doesn't have to be the person you are now. And you don't have to go backwards to make anyone else happy, just yourself."

"I've spent so much time running from what was and fearing what could be," Millie confessed, her voice carrying the weight of years spent entangled in the web of her own hesitations. "But sitting here with you, I realize that perhaps the most courageous thing we can do is confront the unknown with an open heart."

Hayden squeezed her hand gently, a silent affirmation of their shared journey. "Life has a way of surprising us," he replied, his voice a gentle reassurance. "And sometimes, the most beautiful stories unfold when we allow ourselves to be vulnerable, to embrace the uncertainties that come our way."

Snowed in with the Billionaire

A subtle smile played on Millie's lips, a testament to the awakening of a dormant courage within. "I want to discover who I am beyond the echoes of the past," she declared, her words resonating with a newfound determination. "And maybe, in doing so, I'll find a version of myself that I never knew existed."

Hayden, drawing strength from the vulnerability they shared, revealed a layer of himself seldom seen by the world. "I've spent years chasing thrills, mistaking the adrenaline for a sense of purpose," he admitted, his gaze fixed on a distant point as memories stirred within. "But perhaps, in helping you find your way, I'm also rediscovering mine."

Millie's eyes widened with understanding, the unspoken connection between them deepening.

"I've spent so long chasing after the wrong things," Hayden confessed, his voice tinged with a raw honesty that echoed through the small space. "The thrill, the adrenaline—it all felt like a substitute for something real. But in this moment, with you, I'm starting to see that maybe the answers I've been seeking aren't out there. Maybe they're within, waiting to be discovered."

Millie's eyes, filled with a mixture of compassion and understanding, met Hayden's gaze. "It's a journey we're on together," she replied, her voice carrying the weight of shared introspection. "Maybe we're each other's guides through the unknown. And who knows, we might uncover truths about ourselves that have been hidden for too long."

Hayden, his fingers tracing abstract patterns on the surface of the couch, continued, "There's a freedom in letting go, in embracing the uncertainty. It's scary, but there's also a kind of liberation in realizing that the past doesn't have to dictate our future."

Millie nodded, her gaze a beacon of understanding. "It's like shedding an old skin," she remarked, a smile playing on her lips. "And in doing so, we make room for new possibilities, for a version of ourselves that's been waiting to emerge."

Their eyes met in a moment of shared revelation.

"So what's so special about Matt that makes you want to go to him again?"

Millie

"What is it about Matt?"

That's a good fucking question.

"Yes. There has to be something that makes you want to even think about going back with him."

Of course, there were lots of wonderful things about Matt.

That was why she had wanted to marry him…

Wasn't it?

So, why couldn't she think of anything to say?

Maybe it was because their relationship had always been on the quiet side. No grand gestures, no ardent pursuit. He hadn't swept her off her feet. Their love story had been easy, natural—nothing intense about it at all. They had dated for two years, but had known one another since they had been toddlers. They had been pushed together from day one. Because of it, Millie had dated no one else since him. It felt wrong, dirty to think of having another man in her life when she'd spent so long thinking it would only ever be Matt. Even if they weren't technically together, even if he'd told her that he didn't really love her, she could think of no one else.

But what made him special?

She couldn't say.

"I don't know," she replied quietly. She didn't want to think about this, about Matt. She'd spent so long focusing on him, on becoming his wife, on finally pleasing her family. It was all tied up together in her head.

Picking it apart and focusing on just what she felt for Matt was tricky.

"How can you not know? Do you love him or do you not? Do you want to marry him or do you not? Are you going to go home and fight for him, or are you going to just let him walk back out of the door once Christmas is over?"

She was surprised to hear these words coming from him. It almost sounded like support, especially when he continued. "Your mother may have overstepped her boundaries by inviting him without warning you, but if he's the man that you want to spend your life with, then you should take advantage of the opportunity to try to win him back." He smiled, sipping down the last of his coffee, which was probably cool by now. "So, what do you want, Ms. Jeremy? Do you want to marry the man that didn't want to marry you, or do you want to chase him down and show him what he's missing by not marrying you?"

Millie stared at him, taking in his words, trying to process them—and then trying to decide whether to follow his advice or not.

I do love Matt.

At least in one way.

Our love wasn't passionate, but do I need that?

She loved the idea of the life they'd have together—the one where she would finally be able to build a relationship with her family.

She had been reprimanded for not being good enough, for not being who Matt wanted and needed, and Millie had internalized those criticisms, believing that they were right.

She wasn't good enough.

She wasn't strong enough for him.

She didn't have a prestigious enough job to impress his circle of friends.

She wasn't beautiful enough, not classy enough. Her idea of dressing up was a pair of jeans without holes in them.

She cried over everything and had no idea how to stay tough in the face of pressure. She was nearly thirty and still had no idea what she wanted to do with her life long-term. She was a mess, and because of it, Matt had left her. It was what she deserved.

So, with all of that in mind, did winning him back really stand any kind of chance? If he'd realized he could do better than her, she couldn't think of a single thing she could say or do that would change his mind.

Hell, is it even what I want still?

And the sad, silent truth was that while she'd been devastated by the rejection, and by her family's reaction to it, there had also been a small part of her that had been… relieved to not be marrying Matt after all.

"I'm not entirely sure if that's even what I want anymore," she admitted out loud.

She wasn't even aware that she believed the words until she'd actually spoken them. Even if her family had been disappointed and blamed her for what had happened, she had felt relief that she could finally make her own choice. And Matt would not have been it.

Their love story had been too simple, too easy. It had made her sad to think that she might live her entire life without ever experiencing true passion and desire.

Certainly, she never would have found either one with Matt.

"If he isn't who, or what you want, then why spend so much energy on him?"

She let out a sigh. "My parents. I've tried impressing them, I've tried making them proud for my entire life, and always come up short. But Matt was my shot at finally hitting the mark. As his wife, I could finally get into their good graces, so I took that opening and ran with it. When I realized our relationship was cracking apart, I tried hanging on, but I couldn't.

I think that, in a way, I may have once loved him. And still do, just not in that way."

Hayden's head was cocked to the side questioningly.

"Don't get me wrong, he's a wonderful man. Truly. But he isn't the man that I want to be with. Nor am I the woman he wants."

She bowed her head into her hands, humiliated.

"I loved him in the way you love a childhood friend that you share everything with. I love him in the way that you love your protector, your confidant. But I don't think that I ever loved him as a boyfriend, much less a husband. I wanted to, but I never did." She paused. "He knew it too." She was talking to herself more than to Hayden at this point. She let out a low, disbelieving laugh. "He knew, and that's what it was all about."

"He knew? That you didn't truly love him, or that he didn't truly love you?"

"Both, I think. He realized well before I did that, we weren't right for one another."

She replayed their final conversation in her head. The conversation where he walked out of her apartment and never looked back. The conversation that left her curled in a heap on her living room floor, feeling like it was the end of the world. "He tried telling me. Many times. He tried, but I didn't want to listen. I kept brushing him off, telling him that he just had cold feet, that he was nervous." She shook her head, still talking to herself. "I can't believe I didn't see it before."

Even her sister had seen, to some extent, that Matt wasn't right for her. It was odd that, of all people, Hayden was the one to help her to finally open her eyes.

"You clung to him because he was all you knew. It's difficult to do something new when you've always done the same thing. You get comfortable, you get into a routine, and when that routine is disrupted, when everything you know changes, chaos ensues. It's natural to be afraid of that. But the chaos will only hurt you if you let it. Embrace the change and move forward, and you might find that you're better off than you were before. Don't live in your past, Millie."

She started at her name on his lips. She enjoyed it. "You're right. I was afraid. Scared that everything I had known was wrong, everything I had strived for was a failure. My parents undoubtedly called me a failure frequently enough. I didn't want to give them any more ammunition."

There was silence as they both observed the flames. Hayden rose to add another piece of wood and to encourage the flames to continue. Tyler let out a tiny whine and then a huff in his sleep before snuggling up tighter. Hayden grinned down at the dog, his gaze so kind and open that it made butterflies flutter around in Millie's stomach. He looked hot no matter what he was doing—even when he was scowling. But when he smiled, real and natural, it was like nothing else.

He returned to the couch, but only after laying a blanket over Millie, who had begun to shiver. Grabbing a blanket for himself, he sat back down, a bit closer to Millie. "My parents live in Livingston."

"But that's only an hour from here," she remarked, eying him curiously. "You said you have no family."

It was Hayden's turn to show shame. "I haven't spoken to them in five years. When the company took off, I turned away from them and let my primary worry be myself and my career."

She leaned out and placed a touch on his arm. "What happened?"

"Nothing. My folks are beautiful and kind." He shrugged as he looked aside. "Unfortunately, they didn't fit into my plan for success."

The statements sounded like what she would have anticipated from the cynical, calculating guy she'd considered him to be when she'd first arrived on his doorstep, but she'd seen other sides of him now and thought that there must be more to the story. "Your plan for success is to disassociate yourself from your family?"

"No," he answered fiercely, but she could see his expression soften almost as quickly as the word came out. "I'm sorry, I shouldn't have snapped at you. No, it wasn't originally my plan. My plan was to be successful. To never struggle financially like my parents did. My objective was to build a name for myself. And I concluded a long time ago that that meant I didn't have time to squander on a family."

"But aren't you lonely? Spending every morning, every night, every holiday with only yourself? How can you tolerate being so alone?"

Hayden

HAYDEN CLOSED his eyes and faced the flames. He could hear her voice, could feel her words piercing through him, but he wanted to keep them out, to keep them inside his shell. He was unwilling to feel. He was unwilling to consider his family or his history.

I can't talk about this shit.
Why did I come down here again?
Why is she pushing things when we got along so well?
The discussion had come to an end.
He didn't want to talk about this. Not with anyone.
He sprang from the couch and tossed the cover aside. "Miss Jeremy, good night." He approached the steps, but he didn't go up just yet. "Wake me up and I'll rebuild it for you if the fire goes out and you get cold."
"Mr. Dickinson?" she whispered. "Hayden?"
He came to a stop on the steps without saying anything or turning to look at her.
She said softly, "I'm sorry if I offended you with something I said. I simply cannot fathom not becoming a parent, particularly if it is my own decision. However, that is your decision, and I have no authority to assess your circumstances or standing."
He felt an overwhelming need to stay even though she had not asked him to. With a sigh, he let go of the unfamiliar feelings.

Why did it hurt like hell?

He was only concerned with the figures on his bank account, the amount of how many clients he had, and how big the contracts were. He had made the decision to devote himself to that, and it had paid off. It was the life he had always dreamed of.

Everything was flawless.

Yes, it was.

It was necessary; otherwise, what purpose had it served?

Standing at the foot of the steps, he reluctantly thought back to a Christmas Eve twenty years earlier. He remembered hanging stockings, decorating the tree with handcrafted ornaments, and baking cookies in the kitchen with his mother. His father read him a bedtime tale and urged him to go to bed before the sound of the sleigh bells, while he was writing a letter to Santa. He thought back to the wonder of Christmas morning when he woke up and saw the woodland floor covered in white blankets. Running outside to welcome the cold, he would search for indications that Santa had visited the previous evening. Hayden would consistently discover crumbs and footprints.

He thought back to the way he had felt on the inside as well as the outside when his mother would greet him with a hug, put a plate of steaming buttermilk pancakes in front of him, and tell him to finish eating fast so they could open gifts.

He would turn to the tree, which was usually a scraggly Charlie Brown-style tree but was exquisitely decked with ornaments that had been lovingly cared for and kept throughout the years. It never really looked like the elegant trees he'd seen on TV or in department stores. Big boxes were never covered in colorful paper and topped with enormous red bows. However, there were gifts, firmly knotted with twine and hastily wrapped in old newspaper. While that might not have been ideal for some families, for him at the time it was ideal. The only thing he needed for happiness at the time was love.

Snowed in with the Billionaire

Even though the fire was still going strong, Hayden went back to the couch and drew the blanket back over him. The only cold he felt came from inside, from what he was about to tell Millie, as well as to himself.

He began, "My parents were loving and very much in love with each other and cared deeply for me. I never went without love or necessities in my life."

He looked at Millie, who was paying close attention.

"They didn't have much schooling, so for the most part of my life, they worked six or seven days a week at several jobs, often putting in eighteen-hour days per day. I was typically taken care of by the old lady down the street after school and into the evening, so I didn't see them as much as I would've' liked, but I understood why."

Hayden took a deep breath.

"Mom would be the one to come get me after she got home from work because she was typically the first to finish. She would carry me to the car, drive to our house, and then bring me inside and put me to bed. When she wasn't too tired, mom would give me a kiss good night and perhaps read me a story or sing me a lullaby. Dad would arrive home in the wee hours of the morning, right as I was waking up to go to school. Every morning, after making me breakfast, he would divide the comic books between us to read together. He would then shuffle me out the door to school and head to bed in order to rest before starting his next shift."

God this is hard…

Why am I telling her about this?

"I didn't really know them, since I never really got to spend time with them," he went on. "Every day was a challenge for them, even though they worked hard to ensure that I would have all of my requirements met. I used to worry every day about their true nature and why they were unable to support me in the same way that the parent's of my school friends did."

He could feel Millie's eyes on him with what he could only imagine was sympathy, though he refused to look at her.

Even though those experiences were so long ago, he was surprised by how much they stung to revisit. "I wonder who they would, or could, have been if I hadn't been in the picture, now that I'm older and have a greater understanding of the world. If they hadn't had to take care of me, what would they have become?"

Although he was surprised to hear himself say such a thing, he knew the words were accurate even as they came out. He had held himself responsible for their hardship and for his parents' inability to fully enjoy life.

He was an inconvenience.

He had prevented them from experiencing true happiness because they owed their son something.

Millie remained silent, but she grasped his hand strongly. Her hands were small and sensitive, and she exuded warmth. Feeling grateful that she was there, he held her hand tightly. Although it was painful for him to go back in time, he had no idea how much relief he would get from it.

Millie

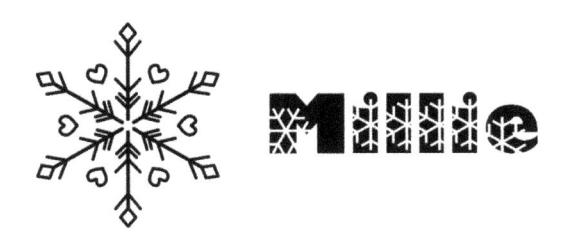

His fingers encircled hers firmly, and his skin was silky and soft. She had a pull at her heart for him as his head sank low.

"But they did love you. Correct?"

"Indeed, their affection was constant. They did everything in their power to make me happy during the brief time we had together, but it was limited because we were never wealthy, we barely scraped by. The cupboard was never fully stocked, the milk was always one day away from going bad, and every other month the power would go out even though they worked almost nonstop. Although we had love, that was really all we had."

All she could say was, "But they loved you."

Hayden furrowed his brows. "They did, indeed."

"I just mean, well, I know that I would much rather have had their love than the material things they provided. I come from parents who rarely, if at all, showed affection." In the hopes that Hayden would comprehend, she hesitated to gauge his response. "We had everything we could possibly want and more, but the love was absent. I would have done anything, and I still would, to win that love."

Squeezing her hand, his contact sent a jolt down her spine. She didn't know what the small shockwave signified, but it made her unwilling to release his fingers. She desired to relive the feeling. She had never had a spark of passion with Matt, despite their years of dating and her belief that she was in love with him.

Nevertheless, she had experienced the much-needed spark here, with Hayden Dickinson.

Had Hayden experienced it too?

He was also observing her, as she glanced up over the rim of her glasses. She could see that his dark, penetrating eyes were focused directly on her despite their shadowy appearance.

Her heart pounded in her ears, her breath catching in her chest.

Had he always been so attractive?

Had she been able to push aside the fact that he was because of her opinion of him?

She could see what other women were attracted to, but as he moved in, brushing her hair from her face, all she could think about was all those women and how she refused to be one of them.

He reached to kiss her, but Millie pulled back just a little. "I apologize, but I can't."

He moved back from her, shrugging his shoulders, without being insulted. "That's alright." He chuckled a little.

She had the impression that there was more to his response than what he was ready to reveal, even though he appeared to brush off the rejection.

She desired a kiss from him.

She desired to feel his arms encircling her.

She couldn't ignore the fact that she was amazed by her own attraction for him.

She was not, however, going to be simply another woman. Not for any man, not for Hayden. "I apologize. I don't want you to believe something negative about me."

"And what is it?"

Her mouth parted, then shut again.

How could I explain to this man that I just avoid having affairs?

"It's alright," he laughed. "I take no offense. I understand."

She grinned gratefully as she leaned back against the couch's arm.

"Would it be possible to move closer so we can stay warm? Since it's getting colder again, I'd prefer not to go outside to bring in more wood just yet."

The wind was banging at the sides of the house, and she could hear it howling. Although the fire was still very strong, she could sense that it would soon die out. Unsure if it was only for warmth or the want to feel his arms around her and his heart pounding against her chest, she pushed herself closer to him. Although she convinced herself it was the first, she was afraid it could be the second.

She was starting to fall for Dickinson's charm.

She cuddled up beside him, putting her glasses on the table so she could easily rub her face against him, and he was more than simply warm. He was becoming hot under the collar.

Or was that her?

She was small enough that his arm encircled her entirely, encasing her like a cocoon. For the first time in a long time, she felt safe. Her relationship with Matt had been so quiet and remote that it had been hard for their private moments to seem truly private, and her parents had never made her feel this way.

She remembered the news story she had heard on the radio that evening, the one about the danger this exact man—who had a protective arm around her—was facing while she considered how comfortable she felt in his embrace. She needed to be aware. She approached the topic cautiously, understanding that if she approached it incorrectly, he might clamp down on her immediately.

She said, "So earlier tonight…" thinking that would be enough to get him to tell the story, but all he did was hum into her hair. "When someone shot at you tonight…" She simply left the sentence hanging there, giving him the chance to fill in the blank.

Hayden sighed, clearly reluctant to do this.

For an instant, Millie believed her question would be fruitless once more.

"I have an idea, but I don't know who it was for sure." Even though she could tell he was uncomfortable talking about it, he persisted. "A few months ago, I got into a fight with one of my business partners about how we should treat a few of our clients. He didn't like the way I was handling things, and he practically lost his job with the company when he didn't follow the rules."

As he forced himself to tell her the details, she felt his body stiffen beneath her. "He has been a part of the business from the start. He's kind of my right-hand guy. He lost a lot of money, and I can understand how someone would get a little insane when they lose that much money."

Her head racing, she gently squeezed him. "Were you injured?"

Hayden laughed. "Something besides Joel knocking me down? No. In fact, immediately after it happened, I was feeling very pumped up. My ego was swollen and my adrenaline was racing. I was shot at by someone? You know, it gave me a sense of importance. Like someone thought enough of me to go to such lengths for me. However, back in the car, with Joel seated across from me in the limousine and Mark still scanning the crowds for the assailant, his eyes were constantly scanning the throng. I had never really given it any thought that I would be killed or that someone might despise me to that extent before the scene and being hurried off to my family cottage. But that's when it all finally clicked, and I did experience terror." The admission almost made him sound ashamed.

She could only shake her head at the peculiar way he

seemed to view the world and the idea that he would be embarrassed to be human.

He kissed her forehead and she closed her eyes, but he did not move. Even though she had rejected his advances just seconds earlier, she couldn't help but feel let down. He put his hand around her back and gently stroked it as she laid her arm across him, letting her hair fall freely across his chest.

Gradually, the light dimmed and the room's corners started to merge together. Was it her imagination running wild, or was the fire going out? She could feel herself blushing from the thought that those lips had been somewhere else. She was simply not that kind of woman.

What if she was, though?

What if she was a risk-taking kind of woman?

Who followed her dreams instead of the values of others?

What if she was the kind of woman who leaped at that moment, her desire too great to resist drawing the playboy to her, reaching up to kiss him?

What would happen if she allowed herself to reach for passion and wouldn't accept anything less?

What if she was the kind of lady who, upon returning home early the following day, declared to her parents that she would finally live her life for herself and no longer for them?

His breathing had slowed against her as she had been lost in her own mind, and she felt a clenching in her stomach. She took one deep breath after another, feeling the quickening thud, thud, thud as her pulse sped. She glanced up at his closed eyes, and at the close range, was able to finally study his features without his piercing stare intimidating her into looking away. His firm jaw, his thick nose that wasn't quite perfectly aligned, as if it had been broken in his past. Tentatively, she reached a hand up to his chin and ran her fingers across the slight show of stubble, feeling it scratch and tickle at her fingertips. He stirred as she traced his jawline up to his cheek and then back again.

She turned to face him, her breast softly touching his chest. He shifted to be next to her, holding on to her. Lifting her head to meet his full face, she could feel his lips brush against hers and taste the last of his coffee, heavy and sweet. She inhaled deeply and leaned in to plant her lips against his. But at the last second, she cursed her cowardice and pulled her head to the side, pressing her kisses to his cheek instead.

In an attempt to avoid waking him up, she carefully withdrew. Even so, he awoke, his hand wrapping more tightly around her lower back to draw her closer to him and bring her up to a height where her lips met his. With drowsiness, he opened his eyes and met hers. He remained silent, observing her. Even though he didn't touch or even look at her eyes, she still felt exposed in his arms.

She waited for him to take the next step, and she became irritated when he didn't. It's just like Hayden Dickinson to control himself and hold back in a situation like this. She had an image of Hayden as the kind of man who would exploit any circumstance. She thought he would be the kind to jump at the chance to take an eager woman into his arms, but yet, here he was, hesitant.

Millie pulled away from him. It seemed that there was a problem with her, as no male, not Matt, Hayden, or anybody else so far, desired to give her the kind of fairytale kiss that she had always secretly desired.

But what the hell?

Why not take the initiative and do some sweeping herself?

She was never going to see him again, she was never going to speak to him again, and she was never going to have to worry about the humiliation of him sending her away. She had as much influence over the issue as he did, so why wait for him to do it?

She leaned closer, breathing in sharply.

Hayden

HER HAND WAS STILL ATTACHED to his chest, the smooth pressure of her body on his, and the aroma of her hair, which was fresh lilac, were all conspiring to send him reeling. It had been a long time since he had experienced such a strong desire for a lady. It knocked him off balance and made him unsure of what to do. He was tempted to feel the texture of her hair by running his fingers through it. However, she had already turned away from the private moment, and he wasn't willing to press it at this point for fear of frightening her away from him.

He was shocked that the mere sensation of her palm on his chest and her lips warm against his face upon waking up could send a shockwave of pleasure through him. Something so simple, but when she withdrew, he let out a mental sigh, wishing she would stay a little longer.

There is something about Millie… something that wants me to know her more.

Something that makes me wish for a forever with her.

When he opened his eyes, he saw that she was observing him and that she had no intention of getting caught.

He tugged her up, as close to eye level as he could. Her breast was pressing against his chest.

God, I wish I could feel her naked body against me.

He maintained eye contact with her, desiring to kiss her. He longed to remove the rude fabric of her top by inserting his finger inside the strap and swiping it over her shoulder, down her breast, baring her to his eyes.

He refrained from doing what he wanted to.

I don't want to force her.

She has to make the moves, or use her words.

God I hope she does!

Her eyes shone brightly in the firelight as she observed him. At the last second, she seemed to give in to what he believed was the same yearning he was experiencing and let her lips wrap around his.

God this woman is giving me a rush.

I want to pin her under me and worship her like the Goddess she is.

He stroked her back and shoulders, making her skin feel as like it was on fire. They tasted each other, her lips burning deep into his. Her shuddering beneath his touch encouraged him to explore her body even more. He knew she wanted it as much as he did when she took hold of one of his straying hands and forced it down to her hip, then her thigh, then between her legs, the heat he felt there blazing at him.

He wanted to take his time with her, even though he was dying to examine every inch of her body. He longed for her to feel valued and desired, to be admired for her true self and her inherent beauty. He wanted her to understand that there was more to it than simply his enjoyment and what he would gain from it. He desired her approval and to make Millie fall apart in pleasure.

Her thighs clenched around his hand, refusing to let go of him. She'd pointed him in that direction, but she didn't seem to be sure what to do, or what she fully wanted. He tried his best to maneuver in the small area while he touched and caressed her thighs through her pants.

Oh I wish she didn't have her pants on. I want to feel that silky smooth skin.

She responded to his touch by spreading her knees slightly and groaning against his lips. Just enough so that he could reach her pussy and he rubbed her through her pants, pressing as hard as he dared. She groaned once again, and for a split second, he was afraid she might shove him away. Rather, she curved into him, accepting his contact.

He moved enough so that he could place her back on the couch's padded seat as he hovered over her. "Are you okay?" he inquired, wanting to be sure this was what she wanted.

With a smile on her face, she drew him closer to her by putting her legs around his waist and her arms around his shoulders. Her little stature in relation to his towering, robust build made him want to treat her gently. It was as if he could crush her with a thought, and he was sure that it might be possible, not only physically, but mentally.

How had I failed to notice her skin's brightness and flawlessness?

How gorgeous and red her lips were, slightly swollen from my mouth meeting hers as I playfully nipped and sucked at it?

He shivered as her fingers plucked at the hairs at the base of his hairline. With his fingers tracing her face, he briefly rested his hand on her cheek while observing her. He wanted to do everything in his power to calm her down because he felt like he was making her anxious.

His fingers found her shoulder and neck, trailing down her side barely sliding across the edge of her breast before lingering on her hip. She drew away from him long enough to take a brief glimpse in his eyes. Even in the faint yellow-orange light emanating from the fire's dwindling embers, Millie's cheeks flushed.

"It's all right, I want this."

He stared into her eyes to see whether her words were true. Her eyes lit up, and he returned the smile by giving her what she desired.

He wanted to take his time with her, and it was taking everything he had to not rush things as he wanted her badly. Step by step, he ran his hand up her blouse, noticing how silky and hot her flesh felt to the touch despite the chilly weather.

A surge of pleasure coursed through his body as she caressed her fingertips across his chest. Hayden felt the pressure of his erection on the fly of his jeans. He slid Millie's shirt over her head, exposing her to his gaze. In a fresh moment of nervousness, she let go of him and instantly raised her arms to shield herself from his gaze.

"Are you comfortable with this?"

He waited as she bit her lip to respond. He would handle this correctly. For him, and for her.

She cocked her head, observing the flames for a brief instant before turning her gaze back to him. "I've only ever dated one individual."

Even though he already knew the answer, he nonetheless inquired, "Matt?"

In return, she gave a nod of approval. "He never saw me. I mean… he never saw me in my underwear."

He needed some time to comprehend her admission. His first thought was that Matt was a complete moron. But then he realized that no male had ever seen her in her underwear. Even though he had only seen the upper part, he had come as close as anyone.

How is that possible?

Her physique was flawless. Her breast were solid and large enough to fit comfortably in his hands without being too small.

God I love that I would be the first.

Wait… Love?

That was a word he had never used. Still, he couldn't go back on his first assumption at this point. He returned her clothing and bra to her. He told her, "I'll turn away," and he did just that.

In a matter of moments, her hand found his arm and he turned to face her once more. She had moved her hand from her chest, and they were bare to eyes.

"I wish for you to see."

Millie

SHE LET him slip her bra over her shoulders, but when she felt herself come free from the support of the under wire, her hands instinctively flew up to cover her exposed breasts. But he turned, averting his eyes, offering her the option to conceal herself from him. By granting her the choice, he was transferring the decision from him to her. She knew he wanted to see her based on the desire-filled expression on his face before he turned away, but he wasn't going to ask for something that knew she wasn't ready to offer.

Millie wanted to give it all to him just because of that—that he was doing this for her, not just for himself. Then she let the shirt fall to the ground, savoring the satin's feel between her fingers, then repeated the action with her bra. She inhaled deeply six times before putting her hand around his arm and turning him to face her. She wanted him to see that she had never been so nervous, and she wanted to give him her entire self. Not just certain aspects of her, for some insane reason.

"I want you to see."

She took his hand in hers and led it to her breast, allowing his fingers to lie on the soft, sensitive skin. Her body throbbed at the touch, his fingers playing lightly, testing her reactions. She'd never thought that she could feel such pleasure from a simple touch, from a small warm breath on her skin.

Her pants button broke as she moved, allowing her to raise her hips and slip out of them. After pulling them down her thighs, he kissed his way back up her body, pausing briefly at her hip before moving to her breast.

Damn it... I want to feel him... all of him.
Why is he taking it so slow?
Wait... is this what it feels like to be worshipped?

Never before has Matt shown her such gentleness or thought about how to make her feel attractive and seductive.

The glacial pace at which he was moving with her tormented her. He taunted her as his fingers went between her now nude thighs, gliding up to her waist and tugging at the elastic of her panties. His fingers moved softly across her folds, his knuckles brushing against her flesh. His fingers moved up and down her seam, working her body up and making her ache for him.

Millie's back arched, anticipating more. She could feel him pressing harder against her thigh, and she was getting impatient to feel him inside her. He responded by pressing his hand harder against her pussy as she pushed her hips higher. She let out a moan as he held her tightly, sensing the pressure building until it cried out to be released.

With such skill, he performed as though he had known her body for a long time before he had ever touched her. He lowered himself to her chest, tracing the curves with his tongue, and then clamped his teeth around one of her nipples. She mixed laughing and moaning at the strange feeling because she wasn't sure which to do. She had never been overcome with such intense feelings.

Millie was finding it difficult to focus on what he was doing because his fingers were still doing amazing things between her legs.

She dug her claws into his back, urging him on. The issue? She desired him to be everywhere. He looked up at her, smiled, and slid between her legs, pulling her underwear off as he went.

Who knew how wonderful this all would feel?

Why did I wait so long to do this?

As he positioned himself between her legs, his tongue darting over her clit, she arched and twisted in response to his mouth showering her with hot kisses as his tongue worked magic. The suddenness of it made her jerk, and she felt Hayden's smile brush against her lips.

"Don't flee from me just yet." Millie felt his moist, hot breast against her delicate skin, which just made her want him that much more.

Millie reflexively tightened against him as his tongue finally made its way inside, both terrified and eager for him to taste her.

His thumb found her hood and pushed it back, rubbing at her gently at first, then picking up speed as she started to follow him. Hayden gave her exactly what she needed, and it was obvious that he enjoyed doing so. His tongue licked up all of her essence, leaving nothing behind as she let out a cry of release.

Hayden moved up and over her, placing himself on his elbows, waiting for her to come back down, kissing her neck lightly. He lifted himself a little, but she could feel how hard he was, so she reached down to touch him. Her suddenness made him gasp, but he willingly embraced her touch.

She released him from his pants, pushing them down as far as she could before lightly touching his cock, moving her fingers up and down its length. She felt the hunger tighten his body over her as her fingers moved over him. His size dwarfed her hand, and she felt herself trembling slightly in expectation of feeling him inside her.

She lifted herself up, impaling herself on his cock slowly, feeling herself stretch around him with a slight pain.

God, this hurts, but the pleasure is so much more…

Why did I wait so long? She asks herself yet again.

She let Hayden take over, pushing just a little deeper, bottoming out in her.

Oh.
My.
God.
He is so deep inside me.

Hayden took his time working with her, gently stroking her cheek, planting a kiss on her lips, and moving his hands over her body. Now that the fire was almost out, and the storm had finally subsided, she could just about make him out in the dull, pale, fractured light of the moon that had found its way through the curtains. All she needed, though, was her ability to feel. Feeling all her muscle tension fade, and relaxed even more with each movement, she trailed her fingertips down his arms.

Her hands became familiar with every part of him as she felt his chest and back, ingraining the image of him in her thoughts. She wished to remember this body forever.

He moved gently, pushing deeply within her with each thrust. Millie retaliated by placing her hands on the couch's arms and using the leverage to push back against him. Every time he pulled out, he would pause before slowly sliding his cock back inside. The whole time looking into her eyes.

This is so much more intimate than I ever imagined!

Her body vibrated with need, and longing just as she could feel his doing. She enjoyed the sensation of his slick, smooth skin against hers and the way his mouth nibbled, sucked, and tormented her neck. She felt him grow thicker inside her, and just as he groaned and began to come in her, she let loose. Their bodies clenched each other tightly.

He gently pulled out of her and rolled them so they could lay side by side. She nestled against his chest as he drew the blanket up over them to protect her from the room's chill.

Do I say something?
Do we just go to sleep?
What is going to happen now?

Hayden

EVEN THOUGH SHE had gone to sleep a long time ago, he was still wide awake and gazing at the ceiling. Millie's eyes were closed against the early morning light as her chest rose in soft breaths.

He reflected back on their conversation and the intimacy they had shared. She would have to depart when daylight arrived. He knew that a part of him would go with her when she eventually left his family's house.

What is it about this woman?

This amazing woman?

I haven't felt this alive in a long time though I'm sure she'll be regretting what we did.

Even though he had spent all night watching Millie sleep, he wasn't tired. He wanted to make sure that she enjoyed her Christmas morning before she left, making him unforgettable. Being here with her, brought him happiness, something that had been missing for a long time. He quickly got up, making sure she was completely covered and still sleeping.

He pulled his pants back on before grabbing his bulky fleece coat and wool scarf, wrapping it around his neck. As he stepped outside he could feel the stinging cold upon his cheeks and ears.

At least the firewood is close.

Though she would be worth it if I froze.

He grabbed a little stack of wood and ran like crazy to

return to the cabin's warmth. As he was ready to step over the threshold and escape the icy wind, he heard and saw the underbrush stirring to his left out of the corner of his eye.

Hayden stood stiffly, waiting to see what it was.

Is it the assassin coming after me again?
Oh god, what about Millie?
Will he hurt her?

It wouldn't take long for someone hiding among the trees with the intention of harming Hayden to understand that Millie would be present for whatever they did to him. Furthermore, if he had been killed, someone could feel compelled to kill her as well. There was a rustle once more, as the dense branches shook off white powder from their limbs, just as a rabbit came bounding out.

Hayden laughed at himself before he turned to walk into the house. Inside, it felt like a sauna compared to the winter storm's piercing wind, even though it was still cool. He made a fresh fire quickly, wanting to make sure Millie was warm enough.

As Millie slept, he observed her with admiration, allowing his thoughts to drift to the picture of beauty he knew was beneath his quilt.

I should decorate the house, really turn this into a Christmas miracle.

Hayden had ignored the attic for years. The boxes he looked for were still piled in the same spot where they had always been when he was a child. He expressed gratitude to his mother for always keeping things where she thought they should go. Making sure not to create any noise, he carried them to the ground floor and started opening each container.

He spent almost two hours decorating the tree and hanging ornaments from its limbs. He was inexperienced in spreading the branches and distributing the decorations evenly. Upon taking a step back to observe his completed project, with the room's lights flickering, he noticed that everything was uneven.

Snowed in with the Billionaire

A tired, raspy voice sounded behind him as he was going to throw everything down and try again, sighing in despair at himself. "It's stunning."

With the comforter pulled over her breast but her shoulders uncovered, Millie sat on the couch.

He gave a tense smile.

Oh god, how long has she watched me?

"Hello, good morning, beautiful." He moved to her side and gave her a cheek kiss. "I figured the least I could do was give you a tree to wake up to since you weren't able to wake up to your family's Christmas tree." He cast a sidelong glance at his six-foot Charlie Brown impostor. "I know it isn't a glamorous tree but it's what I had."

Grabbing his hand, she dragged him down to the couch. "No, it's flawless. I love it."

They watched the lights twinkle together as she rested her head on his shoulder.

He wanted to place a wrapped gift underneath it. Something he could see her tear apart and then beam at when she realized how considerate he had been. He came to the realization that he wouldn't have known what to get her even if he had the time. He had just begun to scratch the surface of all there was to know about her.

He suddenly said, "I think I'm going to see my family today."

He had given it a fleeting thought throughout their previous evening's conversation. But as he sat there with her, gazing at his family's Christmas tree, he had only just decided what to do.

Pushing away from him, she looked at his face. "Really!?" she exclaimed. "Hayden, that's fantastic! I'm sure they'll be ecstatic to have you there!" She gave him a strong hug, and he clung to her for a few extended seconds.

Going home was going to be great, but it also meant he would have to say goodbye to Millie. He would have to watch her disappear from his life and out the door. Maybe into the arms of a different man. His stomach twisted at the thought, which hurt him. Millie, in the arms of another guy. Although he didn't wish for it, he was unable to treat her selfishly.

"Coffee? In addition, I make delicious blueberry pancakes."

It was already moving too fast this morning. Now that she was awake, it seemed like the minutes were passing by too quickly. Previously, he had hoped that she would sleep indefinitely so he could keep her there. It killed him that she might want to go soon.

At his offer of pancakes, she nodded and gingerly pushed aside the blanket to get dressed. He could immediately see goosebumps covering her skin, so he was relieved that he had made the fire for her. He was drawn to her, wanting to see how her silky skin fit into her pants and how her lace bra concealed her nipples. However, he realized she was uncomfortable with his eyes on her. He turned and sauntered toward the kitchen to let her dress without his eyes all over her.

Millie

WHEN SHE WOKE UP, she was disappointed to see the couch next to her unoccupied. Joy swiftly overcame her grief as the lights and tinsel shone at her. Even though Hayden had his back to her, she could tell he had been working long before she woke up by the way he was bent over hanging the final few gold and silver teardrop ornaments. She was somewhat taken aback that she had slept through his skulking, but she was also impressed by what he had accomplished. She could tell he was quite attached to the tree. She wasn't sure if it was because of her or because of the memories of previous Christmas times.

After admiring how carefully he distributed the limbs, she drew the quilt up to her chin and sat back to assess his work. She caught a glimpse of him scowling and retreating to the tree, dissatisfied with the outcome. She wished for nothing to alter on his part. She exclaimed, obviously shocking him, "It's beautiful." It wasn't false.

As he approached her, his face showing his skepticism, he bid her a good morning, and attempted to clarify that he had assumed she would find it enjoyable to wake up to. He was unaware of how accurate he had been.

She saw love and care, something that no one else had ever done for her. She did indeed see love in that tree. Love for the tree itself and what it meant to both of them, rather than love for her in the traditional sense. Millie was very certain that this was the greatest gift she would get this year, even though he couldn't possibly know.

She detested the thought that Hayden would just exist in her mind and that she would be returning home with her family in a few hours. She feared that she would never see him again and would have to live a life without him. If only he would let her explore his limitless depths, she was certain that she had found something in him that she had never expected. She wouldn't have that opportunity after today, though.

She would wait as long as she could until she had no choice but to leave, but he wasn't forcing her out the door just yet.

She was warming to the thought of him witnessing her in all her beauty, but he allowed her to dress in private. She knew that every feature, shape, and flaw would be visible and open to scrutiny, with the sun shining down and filling the room with light.

After getting dressed, she entered the kitchen, where Hayden was putting together heaps of items on the countertop. Over in a corner, Tyler was devouring his meal with tremendous gusto.

"Merry Christmas," he replied, giving her a brief smile.

"The same to you." She chuckled and said, "And wow, you weren't kidding about breakfast. You are aware that there are only the two of us. Three of us, if Tyler can get you to give some of it to him."

Something flickered across his face, vanishing as fast as it appeared.

"I worked up an appetite last night, so I'm hungry."

She imagined them trysting behind the covers, and she felt heat shoot up her cheeks. "Yes, exactly, the same."

"I'm preparing blueberry pancakes with lemon curd, banana compote, and sides of Stilton cheese sausage and applewood cured bacon since we need to commemorate the holiday this morning. We'll have coffee and we'll share mimosas with Veuve Clique."

She was motionless as she took in the richness. "That's just too much."

"Not at all," he said. "We'll consume every morsel, I promise. Still, I could do with a sous chef." Hayden looked at her expectantly.

"Naturally, I'm glad to assist. I'm also skilled in the kitchen, though my menus are usually more on the grits and scrapple side."

He chuckled. "What the devil does scrapple mean?"

She approached him and planted a peck on his cheek. "You don't want to know."

After staring at her for a moment, Hayden picked up a remote control off the counter and pressed a few buttons. Christmas music filled the room in a matter of seconds.

"While I prepare the pancake batter, you can work on the lemon curd."

Millie quickly looked over the counter. "Where is the mixture located?"

He laughed and flung back his head. My name is Epicure. My house is a mix-free zone! Everything is created from scratch."

Millie marvelled at the man who was slowly exposing himself to her as she watched him go to work, sorting and blending. It was unimaginable to her that the giant of business was also a skilled chef. He had obviously spent a lot of time cooking because of the ease with which he handled the implements. He hardly gave the recipe a quick glance. She questioned the number of other women he had prepared lunches for. Given that no one could resist the power of a handmade breakfast, it was a complete woo-move.

"Are you just overseeing or are you also cooking?" Hayden winked while gesturing above the basin with a spatula covered with batter.

Millie jumped when she realized she hadn't touched the pile of lemons in front of her since she had been engrossed in her thoughts.

"I apologize!" She picked up a lemon and quipped, "Aye-aye, Captain."

For a few minutes, they laboured in silence, besides the Christmas music playing in the background, until Millie lost her patience. She was curious to know more about the riddle of the man sucking batter off his fingers just now.

She questioned him, "What's your favourite Christmas memory?"

He responded almost immediately, as if it were a prepared statement for a television interview. "Yes, that was most likely the year that my first business shattered our quarterly records. We had a lavish holiday celebration, and everyone had a great time."

Millie set down the lemon and fixed her gaze on him. "Oh, please, seriously?"

"What?" he asked, expressing real surprise at the rejection.

"It's not that emotional. Tell me a true story."

Hayden fell silent, appearing to be gazing intently at the batter.

He said quietly, "I don't usually talk about this. Because I don't want people to believe that my purpose is to gain attention. Yes, I want people to see a certain side of me for the most part of my life, but this? Yes, but that's only for us."

Millie twitched at the reference to a us.

Who is he referring to as us?

"I choose a different foster child organization each year and get their list. Then everything is signed by my assistant as Santa, so no one can know I'm the one that does it."

Millie felt her eyes well. "Are you serious?"

He gave a nod. "It's the most amazing thing ever, in fact. It hurts my heart how little the kids want. On their Christmas lists, they write items like sneakers without holes and clean socks. It appears as though they are hesitant to request genuine gifts. As you may expect, I give more than what is on their lists."

"With what?"

"Do they desire sneakers? Three pairs are given to them. The newest video games are also included. Does a young child desire a doll? Their new doll comes with matching clothes for her and a whole wardrobe. Do the teenagers want a bike or a skateboard? They receive the best available along with all the necessary safety equipment. I make sure the children know what it's like to experience the wonder of Christmas."

Millie watched with wide eyes as he talked, happiness spreading across his face. "That's amazing," she murmured.

He gave a shrug. "To be honest, I wish I could do more. Well, enough about me. What Christmas memory stands out as your best?"

She struggled to think of anything that could match the enchantment of what he had just revealed to her. She chose not to answer the question. "Well, since we're talking about holiday memories, I should probably give my family a call to check in with them. Give me two moments."

Taking out her now charged phone, she called her parents.

"Hey?" The reply was a bit too upbeat, a little too youthful and lively, a little too naive and friendly. "The Jeremy residence."

I dialed the proper house, right?

She pulled her phone back, double checking.

Yep. So who the hell is picking up my parents' phone?

"Who is this?"

"Oh my God!" The voice asked, hurting Millie's ear with her high-pitched tone, "Is this Millie? How are you doing? We have been anticipating your arrival all morning!"

"Who is this?" she asked again, the woman utterly side-stepping her query.

"Oh my God! I apologize so much! I'm Shannon, Matt's,

uh, girlfriend. Matt has only been raving about your family, so naturally we had to attend when your mother asked us up for Christmas."

Millie's chest and neck burned with hate as she felt her stomach turn over and she was repulsed by it all. "My mother did what?"

Hayden turned to her with concern, realizing that she hadn't meant to say the words out loud. She mouthed, "I'm ok," as she shook her head. She wasn't well, though. She was enraged. Her mother's invitation to Matt had been one thing. As it was, that was insulting enough. To invite the man's most recent girlfriend, though? To repeatedly remind Millie that she was insufficient and that she would never measure up? Millie collapsed onto a seat, feeling queasy.

"Please allow me to speak with my sister."

The woman replied in a mumble. Despite hearing the hurt and bewilderment in her voice, Millie was unable to show her any concern. It was not appropriate for the intruder to be in her house. There was no way Matt belonged in her house.

She waited for a few moments, the rustling in the background hurting like splinters every time. Her sister finally answered the phone and said something in a whisper. "Oh my God, until she showed up with him this morning, I had no idea. I tried to call you on your cell phone, but it wouldn't connect, so I wasn't sure how to get through."

Millie should have been as frantic as Mia sounded. As angry as she would have been the previous evening. But now her mother's cunning tactics were the only thing bothering her.

But before she could soothe her sister, Mia continued to rage. "You need to say something to her. This is too much, she's gone to far. If I were you, I don't even know if I would return home. Never mind about them!"

Millie chuckled at her sister's fit of rage.

"What are you laughing about?" Mia enquired.

"That's alright. I'm okay." Before Mia could say anything, Millie interrupted her to express her scepticism. "I promise, I'm okay."

Mia let out a sigh. "All right, then I'll let it go. However, I'm warning you right now that I will speak with her if you don't. Directly in front of Lola, Matt, Sofia, or whoever the name of that tramp is."

Millie laughed once more at her sister's animosity. "I promise to take care of it." After getting past her initial shock, she was overcome with happiness and couldn't believe how fantastic she felt. Even though it was obviously going to be uncomfortable to be there with the two of them, she found that she wasn't really concerned about it. She genuinely didn't care.

"Alright. When should I let them know, you'll be here?"

Millie cast a sidelong glance toward Hayden, who was in the process of flipping pancakes. Unaware of his appreciative audience, she grinned while he went on cooking. She turned back to her sister and the phone, her grin faltering. "Tell Mom a few more hours, and then I'm heading out of here."

"You do realize that won't make her happy, right? Just letting you know that she has already been causing a lot of trouble this morning due to your absence."

"She will survive. Just let her know that I'll be there whenever I can."

"Well, but it's your ass!" She retreated to a whisper once again. "So, this man? Did anything noteworthy occur there?"

Millie cast a sidelong glance toward Hayden, who remained distracted and oblivious to her words. With her gaze fixed on Hayden's back, she murmured, "We can discuss this later."

"Oh please, hurry up! I need specifics! Whoa, is he in the same room as you?" Her sister laughed. "Is he handsome? Is he nude? Mmm? What attire does he have on?"

"We can discuss this later," she hurriedly repeated.

Mia sighed. "All right, all right. However, we will most certainly talk about it when you get here! Okay, I'll see you shortly."

Millie laughed. "Later, I swear. I cherish you."

"I also love you! Best wishes to you, wink."

Millie moved through the narrow space and stood at the far end of the counter, observing Hayden while he prepared their meal. She felt remorse for her snap decisions the previous evening and was astonished by his level of ability.

"What's going on back home?" After spreading butter and adding syrup, he set the plates on the table with the bacon pieces on the side. "Are your parents disappointed that you haven't returned home yet?"

With a sly smile, Millie answered, "You have no idea. Every year, my mom adheres to this exact timetable. Her plans have been completely thrown off, so she'll probably continue drinking till after the New Year."

Hayden was eating a pancake when he laughed. "And what's the situation with Matt?"

At the mention of his name, Millie flushed. It was because of how much of an idiot she had been, not because she was eager to see him at home. She now understood that her feelings for Matt were but a small portion of what she could feel for someone who actually mattered to her, and if Hayden would ever consent, she believed that he might be that someone. She scowled, realizing he had never made it seem like the kind of guy who would settle down. She was not going to act foolish in front of him twice in a row. "He's already arrived… along with his partner." She didn't feel like laughing because she was thinking about losing Hayden, but she managed a little giggle for his benefit.

He briefly held her hand by extending his arm across the table. The sting it left on her skin and in her heart made her feel nauseous. "I apologize. Will things work out for you?"

She squeezed him reassuringly. "I would have been a

disaster with it yesterday. That being said, I feel very different today."

With a smile, Hayden leaned across the table to give her a kiss. The flavor was a combination of syrup and blueberries, and she kept him there for a while before letting him go back to his breakfast.

Hayden

When he spoke the words, asking about Matt, he didn't think he'd be that concerned with her answer, but as they came out, his gut tightened into a knot.

Her voice was lighter than it had been the last time they had spoken of him, though, when she spoke. Even when she told him that Matt was at her house with his new girlfriend, she did so in a way that suggested it didn't really matter to her. He was overcome with a sense of relief. Though he knew Matt didn't deserve her either, Hayden didn't think he did.

Millie deserved all the love in the world, but any guy who would be willing to crush her heart was unworthy. Though she refused to accept it, Hayden still wanted the best for her.

Even after she had released him, he could still feel her hand pressing against his; as he retreated from her, want still blazed in his mouth. He didn't need to make things tougher on himself, but he felt powerless against her. She looked stunning in the brilliant sunlight, which lit up the room as its rays reflected off the snow's pristine white powder. Her eyes were tired but brilliant and gleaming, and her hair shone in the sunlight. Her skin, still pink and fresh, was beautiful as well. He found it difficult to let her go.

The front door sprang open as two men stepped inside, loose powder billowing in after them. Both of them were well-built and completely clothed in black. The guys moved into the kitchen, their gazes fixed on Millie, and Hayden got up from the table. Before they could perform a thorough body and cavity search, he protectively stood between Millie and his bodyguards because he could already see the fear and suspicion on their faces.

"This is Millie." He turned to face Millie, but he remained in their way. He touched the taller one on the shoulder and said, "Millie, this is Joel. And that's Mark," as he nodded to the stockier, shorter man with a receding hairline.

Although he had previously shocked them with an unannounced female guest, they were aware that he never hosted guests at this residence, and he could also sense that they were still on high alert following the shooting. Even if they were frequently exaggerated when it came to his safety, he was grateful to have them at his side.

"Is everything alright?" Mark looked at Millie as he inquired.

"Not really," was his response. "This young woman refuses to eat her breakfast. Declares that she is full."

Mark eventually smiled as his guard broke. "Is that true? Well, were the pancakes burned?"

Hayden shot back, angry, "Excuse me. You know me better than that."

Millie laughed and remarked, "I'm stuffed. But it was all really wonderful. There are lots of leftovers here." She looked at Hayden with hope.

"Yes, gentlemen, that is correct. There are plenty of pancakes remaining in the kitchen, so please feed yourselves. After all, it's Christmas."

After they went into the kitchen, he came to the realization that his time with Millie was coming to an end.

"After I leave here, will you have them take you to your parents?" Millie inquired.

He reclined in his chair, on the back two legs; the breakfast having given him a sluggish feeling following his lackluster sleep the previous evening. "Yes, I believe I will. But I would want to make a couple stops for gifts."

Years had passed since he had sent any Christmas gifts, though he had sent several in the first few years after cutting his ties with his family. Each year, they had given him gifts, but he had declined to give them back. He hadn't even sent them a card, and he was starting to feel bad about it.

He owed them an explanation.

Millie's dejected expression baffled him.

Is she not pleased that I'm going to visit my family?

I thought she would be happy I was.

"Hayden, the fact that their son returned home for Christmas is all that your parents will need. That's all they've ever actually wanted from you, I'm sure of it. Not to mention, no retailer will be open on Christmas Day. Everyone else in the world is with their families."

He started to say that regardless of the day or time, doors always opened for him, but then he stopped.

That was not the purpose of this day.

Not any longer.

All he wanted for Christmas was time with the people who meant most to him, so he knew she had to be right. His family and, should he be telling the truth with himself, Millie, too.

"Considering Christmas and family, you ought to be preparing to return home, don't you?"

Though he didn't want her to leave, he also wouldn't keep her around for longer than she desired. He was aware that she desired to spend the day with her family, and he planned to assist her in returning home.

Millie

Though her heart was hurting and her head was pounding, he was clearly telling her it was time to leave.

He must not want me here any longer and wants to get about his day. What did I expect to happen?

She picked up her things after breakfast and cleaned without thinking.

Hayden instructed his men to accompany her to her car and assist her in starting it. Peering out the windows, she noticed them standing next to a beautiful black truck in the driveway, providing them privacy as they said their goodbyes.

She closed up her purse and felt Hayden observing her from across the room. Even though she was feeling depressed, she tried to lighten the mood with a joke, "Guess I'm a light packer."

Since he obviously didn't feel the same way she did about their time together she was unable to let him understand how profoundly the last twelve hours had affected her.

The fact that the manner he had held her had seemed so authentic and real didn't matter.

"Yes."

She waited for him to elaborate, but he said nothing. She could only image how eager he was for her to be gone. She made a gesture over the large room as she continued, "Well, thanks for... everything. You pretty much prevented me from freezing to death."

"How could I not?" Hayden enquired, but his speech came across as stiff and formal.

"I wish you well with your family," she stated, staring at him. She still wanted what was best for him, even when it felt like he was brushing her off. She wished he would take her advice and get back in touch with his family. "It will be fantastic."

His hard exterior crumbled, and something inside him seemed to change. It seemed as though he had at last been reminded of the unique bond they shared. Their hearts may have thawed due to the festive charm, even though the storm had forced them together.

"Millie...I'm grateful for everything."

Her eyes widened. "What do you mean?"

Hayden moved across the space, standing close to her. "You forced me to consider some issues that I hadn't been ready to for too long. Thank you for that."

Millie had to force herself not to leap into his arms as they gazed at each other. But she knew that he desired his former life—the one without any room for anything but work.

Their evening together would remain only a priceless memory.

"What do you know? Hayden Dickinson, you're an outstanding dude. Though I was mistaken, I believed I knew you."

He grinned. "Will you make sure everyone knows that I'm actually nice, clear the record I have." He tried to keep a straight face but a laugh escaped him.

There were things unsaid that charged the air in the room. Millie stuffed her hands into her pockets to resist the need to touch him. There was no reason to add more time to the pain of saying goodbye.

Millie slung her handbag over her shoulder. "Alright. Well, farewell then."

Snowed in with the Billionaire

Hayden inhaled deeply. "I'll miss you, Miss Jeremy. It was a joy to meet you."

Before she could do something she would later regret, she turned and hurried to the door. She would not attempt to make any kind of physical contact with him only to have him reject her. The enchantment was broken. It was a fresh day, the storm had passed, and the sun shone.

She needed to focus on the conflict that was about to happen at her parents home.

Her cheeks were painfully cold, and she quickly lost sensation in her fingers and toes as she hurried to the truck. Her sneakers were no longer wet from the previous night, but it only took six steps to get them wet again. She moved to the truck, letting Joel assist her inside, and they drove her the short distance to the ditch where her accident had occurred.

Her car was freed from the ditch in a matter of moments, and she was soon driving again. She turned on the radio to try to divert her mind, going back to the station where she had first heard about Hayden. But she was bored with the morning radio announcers banter very quickly. All she could do was keep imagining a life with Hayden.

The hours in the car seemed to go by quickly. Millie zoned out for long spans of time, only to realize with a start that she was passing another landmark that would eventually lead her to her parents house.

Maybe I should just keep driving to avoid all this mess.

SHE ENTERED HER PARENTS' home softly, knowing full well that everyone was gathered around the tree in the formal living room, munching on cookies. She was not yet ready to put up a front for them. Millie proceeded directly to her room and shut the door. She fell onto her bed and looked at her childhood belongings. That her mother had actually kept the bulk of it intact was truly miraculous. Now that she was out of the house, she had expected the room to be converted into an exercise area or a craft room. The shelf holding plush toys, the mirror displaying pictures of her and Matt, and her few medals and trophies—none of which were for first place—all belonged to her. Only further proof of the ways she had let her parents down.

Shutting her eyes, she gave in to sleep and dreamed about the one night she would always remember Hayden.

The sound of a gentle knock on the bedroom door cut short her dreams, which she would have rather to remain in than face the day. Millie sighed and crossed the room to the door, pulling pictures of herself and Matt off the vanity.

Where did the damn trash can go?

She tossed the pictures on the bookshelf by the door as she flung the door open, revealing Matt. She waited for a surge of feelings, but she had none.

"Hello, unknown person." He looked her over and said, "I saw you come in, but you just blew through without saying anything. Are you alright?"

She had imagined what it would be like to see him again, and the reality was far different from her mental picture from the day before. Unexpectedly, she didn't feel the emotions she was expecting to, like yearning and missing him and hoping for a reunion. Of course, he looked amazing, Matt usually did. However, it was in a fussy, boyish fashion, with excessively coiffed hair and an ensemble that appeared more costume-like.

She was unable to determine whether the ugly Christmas sweater he was wearing was an ironic gift from her mother or if it was a genuine item.

"Yes, thank you. I'm okay." She said as she turned to return to her bed, "I'll be down in a bit."

Snowed in with the Billionaire

Matt followed her into her room. "Look, I understand that you might not want me here, but your mom asked me to come. I know that you might feel a little awkward having me here, but I think it's crucial that we stay friends."

Millie shot him a perplexed glance.

He went on, "I'm sorry that things between us turned out the way they did. But since I am practically as much a member of this family as you are, we must figure out a solution that will allow you to control your emotions. I hope that one day you will be able to move on, just as I have. You don't have to feel the same way about me, but I want you to know that I'm pleased right now. With Shannon."

Millie scowled. "What are you even talking about?"

She was disgusted that Matt would think she was still in love with him, but he seized her hand in his before she could correct him. She balled her fingers into a fist to prevent him from thinking that she enjoyed his touch because his grip was as tight as a vice.

"I need you to know that I'm not the one for you, but you'll find someone when the time is right. I apologize. I am aware that you have found it difficult to handle this. You probably assumed that we would have time to work things out when you heard that I would be here for Christmas, but that is simply not going to happen." He stopped, and she could see he was having difficulty finding the right words. "Shannon and I are..."

God, he really thinks I'm hung up on him. I MIGHT have been but Hayden cured me of that. How did I never see how much of a sniveling asshole he was?

He responded softly, as if he were worried Millie would break down in tears upon hearing the news, "I think you should know that Shannon and I are engaged."

She responded, "Congratulations, I hope you two will be very happy."

His shocked expression gave her a small sense of success.

"We most certainly will be. She is perfect, unlike when you and I were together." With that final dig, Matt withdrew from her room.

Millie grabbed the pictures back up and walked them over to the trash can she had seen as Matt had been talking and threw them out, glaring at them before deciding it was time to head downstairs, join her family, and face the music. They were gathered in the living room, with the exception of Mia, who was hunched over the kitchen stove. Christmas dinners had not been prepared by their mother ever since Millie and Mia had reached adulthood.

Mr. Jeremy was fast asleep in his recliner, and Mrs. Jeremy was already sipping on a cocktail. Mrs. Jeremy was seated across from Matt and Shannon, and the three of them were chatting.

Shannon was stunning, no doubt about it. She was tall and thin, with blue eyes and beautiful blond hair, but she also wore more makeup than was necessary. Her scarlet dress, which was way too thin for the winter months in the north, was knee-length. However, Millie was tactful and introduced herself before turning to face her mother, who held up her glass for Millie to refill rather than giving her the traditional greeting.

She muttered where Millie could barely hear, "It's about time you got here." Louder, she said, "Happy you could be here to bless us with your presence, my love. We've postponed our whole Christmas to be with you. Could you imagine how much work I've done today? Cooking, cleaning, and decorating? But that's our selfish Millie. Correct, Matt?"

"Oh, I'm not aware of that," Matt said, becoming a little awkward.

Shannon smiled at her empathetically.

Without further comment, Millie pivoted on her heel and made her way to the kitchen. Letting her mother get sober would be the worst plan of the day. In actuality, after a few drinks, she was more tolerable. It made it such that when she inevitably tripped over something invisible, Millie could laugh at her with impunity.

She slammed the glass on the kitchen counter and yelled, "Hey, you," at her sister. "Would you like to give me a hug?"

Mia quickly finished taking out a tray of sugar cookies from the oven before she tossed it on top and embraced her sister.

"Oh, I'm so glad you're here! It was more than I could take!"

At last, Millie let out a giggle and embraced her sister. Everything was always better with Mia around. With her hair styled in a flawless bob, her sister was stunning as usual, but Millie could see the weariness in her eyes.

"I apologize. If I could have, I would have spent last night here."

She was actually relieved that her car had become lodged in a ditch. It was not as though she would be returning home to the comfort and happiness of her loving family. The hell she was going to get out of her mother for the rest of the day had been worth her evening with Hayden.

"Yeah, you missed a lot of great family time," Mia rolled her eyes. "Incessantly fleeting moments."

Millie chuckled. "Mom's cheeks are bright pink, but she's still pretty with it," she remarked, using their mother's level of inebriation as a benchmark. "How much time has she spent drinking?"

Mia gave a shrug. "I have no idea; I've been in here cooking all day."

Millie let out a sound of disdain. "I bet she's going to claim the glory for all of your efforts. She's a miserable creature."

She gave a shrug. "Yeah, that's nice. It's quiet in here since she doesn't come in."

They looked at one other, sharing the sentiment that they should both push their mother to drink more. Since they were small children, alcohol had always been a part of their lives, and they had both discovered that their mother was easier to get along with after a few drinks. Her incessant criticism was reduced to a level they could put up with. She wasn't a joyful inebriated; rather, it seemed as though the booze neutralized every negative trait they detested in their mother. Even yet, they could easily divert her attention to less painful subjects while she was intoxicated. They would still receive criticism for their attire and inquiries about their weight.

"She had a fit last night about you. Given how much she talked about you being away, you would have assumed that you had planned the storm and the car accident. I tried my best to run interference for you, but she wouldn't have it. You made the ideal little false family she had in her imagination impossible, and you know she wants what she wants when she wants it. It had to be all of us or nothing, so she couldn't upload any Christmas Eve pictures to Facebook to brag to her pals."

Millie realized she hadn't eaten since breakfast at Hayden's place, so she grabbed a green bean and shoved it in her mouth. She suppressed her grief.

"Have you chatted with Matt yet?" Mia enquired.

Millie grinned then giggled as Mia arched an eyebrow and said, "Yes, he came up to my room."

"He did what?!"

"Not at all like that. He approached to ask if we could be friends." Millie laughed again, even louder this time. "He wanted me to know that he and I are definitely over and that he is moving on with his life. He thought I was building him a shrine or something when he came in right after I was throwing out all of the pictures of us."

"Wait, discarding them?" Her sister gave her a sceptical look. "Are you genuinely moving on from him? At last?"

Millie reddened as she considered Hayden.

After spending time with Hayden, how could I ever entertain the thought of Matt?

"No, I'm not just moving on from him. I'm done with him."

"It seems that you had a great night!" Mia gave me a wink.

"Later. I had better get this over to Mom before she yells at me."

Gazing at her sister, Mia narrowed her eyes. "Yes, I do not want her to be micromanaging me here. Your tardiness has already caused Mom to become irritated. Don't ignore her; that will only give her more motivation to torment us."

Although Millie rolled her eyes, she knew Mia was correct. Christmas was not a time for family fun, but rather for their mother to be pleased. "Give her ten minutes, and then get your ass back in here. I'm going to require assistance getting items out of this disorganized kitchen."

Shannon and Matt were listening to her mother's regaling with rapt attention. Millie set down the drink and sank into the chair that was furthest away from her. The three carried on talking as if she didn't exist, which made her feel uncomfortable, out of place, and unwanted in her own parents' house. She sagged further into the chair as her father's gentle snores lulled her to sleep.

In response to her mother's droning voice, Shannon cackled.

Was mom really that hilarious?

Though she didn't think so, Matt and Shannon were consuming every word.

Her mother yelled, "Millie! Did you hear me just now? Are we keeping you up?"

"What?"

Mom let out a sigh. "Why didn't you dress nicer? You

appear to be a housekeeper. Just look at how stunning Shannon is. That is how the holidays are observed."

"I arrived late. I think I was mistaken when I assumed that joining you would be more essential than getting dressed well."

Her mother retorted loudly enough to startle her father, "Yes, you are wrong. You'll have to change soon since we need to take pictures. Could Shannon perhaps assist you with your cosmetics and hairstyle? You constantly seem like a ghost because you never wear enough. Could you help Millie get ready for the pictures?"

It was the last straw.

"That is ENOUGH!" Millie bellowed, causing the room to become quiet. "Please, I don't need to be fixed up. This isn't a trip to Buckingham Palace; this is a family meal. In addition, Mom, what on earth are the non-family members doing here?" She gestured to Matt and Shannon, who appeared equally as surprised by her outburst as she herself was. "I'm not with Matt now, and we never will be. Why is he in my home, celebrating Christmas with my family when he is not and has never been a member of this family?"

Her mother pretended to be shocked, acting quite shocked and worried about Millie. "I assumed you would be delighted to see Matt and get to know his future wife? I don't know why you're feeling so angry. He has always been a member of our family. The mere fact that he found someone else does not change that."

She snapped back, "Well, it should, because it's weird. Shannon, Matt, shouldn't you be spending today with your own families?"

Both of them drew in closer to the couch, appearing uneasy about being singled out.

Matt began, "Well, I thought it would be nice."

"Nice? To what, show off the ring you gave Shannon? Do you want to try to bring me down on myself?"

He winced.

"Shannon, how about you? I can't believe you are really here. How strange is it, really, to spend time at the home of your fiancé's ex-fiancé? It feels crazy just saying those words!"

Even her father turned to stare at Shannon.

With downcast eyes, Shannon murmured softly, "Well, it wasn't exactly my idea."

From across the room, Millie could practically feel her mother's glare. She could tell that the woman was getting ready for a fight because of the way she was grasping her tumbler and sat rigidly in the chair.

Finally, she lost it. "You're not going to come in here pointing fingers like that, and it's not Matt's fault that he isn't a part of the family. If you had only done what was expected of you, had you only been the woman that your father and I raised you to be, that Matt needed you to be, this wouldn't have happened." She turned to Shannon and said, suddenly friendly, "I mean no disrespect to you, sweetheart; you are adorable. I only mean that things may have turned out very differently for my daughter if she had been half the lady that you are."

Shannon's hands were folded in her lap when she looked down.

Millie watched in disbelief as her mother tried to correct her. "We haven't asked for much from you, but the one thing we did expect—look at what you've consequently lost," her mother shook her head. Very disappointing. You'll never be anything but a barista," her mother said, waving her hands in the air to find the right phrase, as though the idea of it were bothersome. "If you don't sort out your priorities and quit being so obstinate, you'll be alone forever! When you're so independent, what man will desire you? Shannon may be able to teach you a little thing, similar to learning how to be a true woman!"

The final words reverberated like a slap throughout the

space. Millie noticed that Mia had emerged from the kitchen and was waiting for her in the dining room shadows, ready to jump to her defence at a moment's notice.

She didn't require her sister, though. She felt empowered to confront her mother's insanity on her own for the first time.

"Maybe, Mom, I'm not what you consider a true lady. Perhaps I don't want a man who would hold me to that standard. I believe there is someone out there who will love me just the way I am, and I like myself just the way I am."

Her mother's face changed from one of rage to shock. She looked around the room to see how Millie's response was going, and it appeared like her mother was attempting to think of what to do next.

Millie had always prepared for her mother's outbursts. When she was younger, she would simply bow her head and take all the jabs as they came at her, trying to find something else to focus about. Grown Millie had had enough. She refused to allow her mother to spoil one more holiday.

"Do you realize how embarrassing you are?" Despite the lack of support in the room, her mother sneered and showed that she was not about to back down. "Your father has stated as much as well."

Matt and Shannon moved around on the couch, obviously wishing they had not decided to join the Jeremy family for their holiday.

Her father entered the melee at last and yelled, "Now hold on there. I didn't say that at all."

Millie realized it was real. Although her father was not as supportive of her as her daughters were, he would never have said something so blatantly hurtful, and he wasn't going to let his wife lie about it either.

She shot him a slur in return, "Well, I'm sure you think so."

"Also, your sister."

In the mood for combat, Mia hurried into the room.

"Pardon me? Mom, are you kidding me? Millie and I are best friends, as you are aware. Try not to set us against one another; it will not succeed."

Suddenly, her mother appeared to understand that she was outnumbered and that everyone in the room was observing and evaluating her. She pushed back into the chair and screamed. "Why are all eyes on me?"

Millie muttered, "Because we can't believe that we let you ruin another Christmas. Mom, this is not what any of us want."

With a sarcastic tone, she questioned. "Well, why don't I just vanish if I'm that bad? Would you be content with that? When others inquire about my vacation, I'll simply go cry in my room and tell them exactly what you guys did to me." She spilled wine on the floor as she fought to get out of the chair, then tipped back the remaining drink and banged the empty glass hard against the end table next to her. When she stormed out of the room, nobody attempted to stop her.

Staring after her mother, Mia mumbled, "Well, Merry Christmas to you, too."

"I believe it's time for us to depart," Matt remarked, projecting a surprised expression.

Millie responded, "Yeah, that's probably a good idea."

Despite her need to hold onto her anger, she realized that Matt had been more incompetent than malicious. It felt normal to him to turn up for the Jeremy family's Christmas celebration. Hopefully, he now realized how uncomfortable it was and how unnecessary it would be for him to stay there in the future. He didn't have to be a part of Millie's family; he and Shannon could start their own. Shannon grabbed his hand as she led him outside. As she left, she gave Millie a pitying smile, and Millie couldn't help but feel a bit sorry for her. Shannon wasn't at blame for becoming entangled in the chaos.

Her father remarked, as if what had just transpired was

unimportant, "Well, girls, that's that. Do we now unwrap the presents?"

Millie gave a headshake. As usual, he was emotionally absent-minded, but at least he made an effort to maintain order.

"Not just yet, no." She replied, "I think I want to go for a walk and cool off."

"Do you want me to join you?" Mia enquired.

She smiled tightly as she met her sister's gaze. "No, thank you; I'm fine. I won't be out for long."

Millie went to the front hallway and got her coat on. She glanced in the long hallway mirror and saw herself.

She was dressed in the same clothes as the day before, so it didn't take long for her to understand that her mother was right. She really did look like a cleaning lady. Reaching over her ears, she pulled her hat down. It was quickly getting darker outside, and the day would soon be cold.

Her parents lived on a cul-de-sac where every house appeared to have been professionally set adorned for the holidays.

The one on the left had glittering snowflakes all over it, while the house to the left had two enormous nutcrackers standing guard by the door. She was relieved to get outside because she had been feeling stuffy inside the house. The air was bitterly chilly.

Glancing past the houses, she looked in their windows as she went. She saw the contented families enjoying each other, and it was difficult not to feel a little depressed. There was a group in the next house dancing about, and another group eating at a huge dining room table. She even caught the silhouettes of a couple cuddling up against the blinds.

Millie let out a groan and sank her hands farther into her pockets. She was alright. Up until the next outburst, her family would get up the following day, act as though nothing had happened, and carry on as usual.

She had her sister, at least.

It had felt for a little while that she might finally be able to count on someone else to support her.

Hayden.

The previous night began to feel even more like a dream as the hours went by. It appeared unreal.

He appeared unreal.

The Hayden Dickinson she had envisaged was not at all the person she had met. Other than his public demeanour, he was kinder, sillier, and sweeter. She pictured herself as one of the select few who had the good fortune to see the actual man behind the tabloid picture.

She didn't notice the footsteps approaching from behind her until they were almost on top of her since she was too preoccupied with her feet digging into the snow.

"Happy Christmas."

Millie whirled around, startled to see that someone else was not with their family gathered around the tree, but rather out in the cold.

It couldn't be. He was supposed to be at his family's. He couldn't possibly be on her street, dressed for a formal occasion in a black cashmere coat and a bright crimson scarf.

"Hayden? How? How come you're here? Why?"

The realization that the man she had been daydreaming about was just a few feet away from her was so overwhelming that she was unable to articulate complete phrases.

Millie felt warmth shoot through her when he grinned.

He continued to smile and replied, "I'll answer your questions in order. First question: Yes, it is indeed me, Hayden. The second question: how?" He gestured to the identical black truck that had left her off at her car earlier that morning, just over her shoulder. "I have the tools at my disposal to locate anything and everything. It was easy to find the address of your parents. The third question: why? Though I'm robbing you of your family on this momentous day, I'm hoping we may have a little conversation."

Millie smiled as she lifted her hand, hiding the fact. "And why is that?"

Hayden approached her and gently took hold of her arms; his hands were so large and powerful that she could feel the pressure even through her heavy down coat. Her pulse tripled in rate while she turned to face him, curious to see what else he would say.

"Why?" he said again. "Millie Jeremy, you did something to me, which is why I'm here. You have captured my imagination like no one else in less than a day. To be completely honest, you also made me a little insane, but I still enjoyed it."

The recollection of how their evening had started made her blush, and she laughed.

"Millie, I don't want what we've started to stop. Making pancakes for you is something I want to do more lazy mornings. I want you standing there with me the next time I decorate my country house with a Christmas tree," Hayden paused and glanced up at the sky, then around the street. "I hope you feel the same way—we have much to discover together. Ugh, when you need mistletoe, where is it?"

Millie plucked him by the collar. "I don't need an excuse to kiss you." She raised herself to her tiptoes and kissed him. She knew it hadn't been a dream the moment they kissed. Every last moment of happiness spent with Hayden had been genuine. He seemed desperate for her, as if he was also in disbelief that she was back in his arms.

When they separated at last, Millie's eyes widened. "Hold on, wait. Why aren't you spending this Christmas with your family?"

"Don't worry—that comes after. Tyler is currently being boarded at the veterinarian's office, and I have a charter waiting for me at the airport. Despite its diminutive size, the plane can accommodate two people." He squinted at her. "I wish I could kidnap you and carry you away with me. You would be adored by my parents. I would love for you to meet them."

Millie went through the options in front of her while he put his arms around her in a bear hug. She had the option to remain for more of the most awful Christmas party ever or toss everything in and go into the sunset with a man she hardly knew but who she already knew would soon become her everything.

With a gentle nod, she leaned her head against his velvet lapel and whispered, "You can."

"What can I do?" Hayden mumbled against her head's crown.

"Kidnap me. You have my personal invitation to do so."

Leaning back, he gazed down at her, hope shining in his eyes. "Are you serious?"

Millie gave a nod. "Yes, very serious. The only problem is that none of my valuables were packed. All I have with me are trousers and a couple of elegant tops. I don't feel comfortable being around your folks in such simple clothes."

"Stop that. They won't give a damn, that's not who they are. Hold on, though—do you really want to spend Christmas Day apart from your family?"

"Oh, do I ever!" She smiled glumly at him. "They'll understand, I promise. My sister, on the other hand, is the only person whose viewpoint I really care about. She will, if anything, feel envious that she is unable to attend."

She laughed with glee as he whooped and tightened his grip, spinning her around. "Millie, that's incredible! Is it possible for us to go soon?"

"This minute."

Once more, Hayden moved in to kiss her, sweeping her back into a dramatic clasp. When he eventually got her back up, she seemed a little lightheaded.

Millie clutched his arm and murmured, "I can't wait for our next tomorrow," as they made their way to the car.

"Feel at ease, Miss Jeremy." Hayden squeezed her even harder, as if to demonstrate that the fairy tale was only getting started. "I think we have a lifetime of them to come," he added.

Epilogue

MILLIE LET OUT a cry and hurled a snowball towards his head. Tyler jumped up and barked as Hayden dove just in time to see the item splatter against the side of the cabin under a huge evergreen wreath.

"You throw like a girl," he made fun of her.

"Oh yeah?" inquired Millie. "Watch this."

She bent down, grabbed a handful of snow, rolled it into a ball, and threw it at Hayden before he could react. The blow to his chest was so strong that he moaned.

"Well, okay, I apologize," he said, laughing as he gripped the area where it had struck him. "Truce?"

"What did you say?" With a victorious grin, Millie asked. "I can't hear you."

"Please, Truce!"

"Ok, fine, I feel a little cold, perhaps it's time for us to go inside anyway. Somewhere over here, I lost a glove. Could you please help me find it?"

"Yes," he said as he crossed the snow-line separating his and her battlefields.

Millie laughed mystically as soon as his foot touched her side, bending over behind the small snow barrier she had constructed. She picked herself up, two snowballs in each hand, and threw them at him with such ferocity that he fell to the ground.

He smiled, "No fair, we agreed on a truce," as Tyler charged at him.

Millie rushed over and knelt down at his side. "But I'm sorry, sucker; I didn't consent to it. In battle and love, all is fair."

Grabbing her sky-blue scarf, Hayden drew her down onto his chest. "I think we have about the same amount of both."

She scowled. "No, our relationship is not at war. Sure, disagreements. Naturally, arguments. But never, ever go to war."

After drawing her all the way down to him, Hayden repeatedly tied her scarf around his hand. He then reached up to bridge the gap so he could kiss her. "That was definitely not how it began. It still amazes me that a year has passed. The moment I first saw this stunning woman."

"Oh, kindly. I believe your initial reaction upon seeing me was to slam the door in my face." Millie fell back on his chest, laughing. "What an asshole you were!"

"All right, I admit that I wasn't at my best. However, didn't I get friendlier later on?"

"Yes, you most definitely did,"

After a few minutes of kissing, she lowered her lips to his and the cold began to seep through Hayden's down parka.

"Can we move this inside, please?"

Leaning forward, she extended her arm to grasp his hand and lifted him up.

The previous year had gone by quickly, and there were times when Hayden still found it hard to believe that he had a happily ever after at his doorstep thanks to a strange snowstorm and a turn of events.

He never would have needed to be in the cabin if the gun hadn't gone off at that gala. He winced to consider what might have happened to Millie on that wintry evening when she trudged up his cabin's long driveway only to discover it was empty.

Snowed in with the Billionaire

It felt like Millie had always been a part of his life within a week of their first meeting. Yes, it took some time for her to get used to the comforts he took for granted, but he relished her amazement at his magnanimity. He once said the two magic words, no limits, while taking her shopping. When she had bemoaned about the long, dark winter, he had flown her to Santa Barbara for the weekend. That one time when he sent stylists and makeup artists to their house to get her ready for a gala at work. Because she never expected anything from him, he loved indulging her.

"Ooh, it feels so good in here," she said, slipping off her coat just inside the front door.

Hayden paused to admire her. There were no more ripped jeans and ratty sweatshirts. Millie looked après ski ready in slim fitting black all-weather pants and the blue and white patterned sweater they'd bought in Switzerland.

She turned and caught him staring. "What?" she asked, smiling at him.

"You," he muttered. "You're so damn beautiful."

Millie dropped her head and looked bashful. "Stop."

"Never." Hayden shrugged off his coat and tried to calm his nerves. "Want something to warm you up?"

"Yes, please. I'll take a glass of SOMETHING TO WARM THEM UP ALCOHOLIC, and I'll meet you by the fire."

Hayden jogged to the kitchen, happy to have something to focus on other than what was about to come.

They had a full schedule planned the next day for Christmas, welcoming guests from both of their families. Even though he could negotiate deals in three languages he still felt nervous every time he thought about trying to juggle all of the personalities. But he'd put his business acumen to work, setting up events for them to focus on throughout the day, like sledding and making s'mores by a bonfire. His relationship with his parents was back on track after a few heart-to-heart conversations, but Millie was still finding space in her heart to forgive her mother. After the disastrous Christmas the year before, they realized that something had to give, and the pair had slowly worked their way to a more stable version of a mother-daughter relationship. It wasn't perfect, but it was better than it had ever been thanks to therapy.

His hands shook a little as he poured their drinks. He was still getting used to the hosting stuff. Actually, wanting to have people around was a new sensation for him, and he had Millie to thank for it. At first, he'd tried to delegate the Christmas day prep to staff, but Millie had gently reminded him that they probably wanted to be with their families for the holidays. Plus, she'd told him that they didn't have to impress anyone. All that mattered was being together and making memories as a family. They'd prep the turkey, various casseroles, vegetables and desserts as a team, laughing their way through all of it.

Hayden took a long draw from his glass of whiskey to steady himself, then walked back into the great room.

"Hey, Millie? Where are you?"

"Over here." Millie's voice was husky and Hayden immediately knew what it meant.

He glanced around the room eagerly.

"Look down."

Hayden walked closer to the massive fireplace and nearly dropped the drinks.

"Holy shit, woman!"

Millie was naked beneath the very blanket they used the night they made love for the first time. The blanket was positioned low on her back, barely covering her ass, with the two dimples he loved peeking out. She was propped up on her elbows with her forearms strategically placed so he could see the swell of her breast but not her nipples, and her bare feet were kicked up behind her playfully.

There was a red bow on top of her head.

"Merry Christmas, baby. Do you like your present?"

Snowed in with the Billionaire

The fire turned her skin golden, and he longed to run his finger down her back, to trace kisses along her spine until she giggled and moaned. He felt pressure building but he shook his head.

Millie scowled. "What's wrong?"

"Absolutely nothing. My life has never been more right. But I need to focus for a minute."

She sat up, giving him a tantalizing glance of her bare breast before pulling the blanket around her shoulders.

"I'm listening…" she said with a worried expression, always ready to give him the space he needed to express what was on his mind.

But this time, she had no idea what was coming.

Hayden dropped down beside her, so close that their shoulders touched. He always wanted to feel her nearby. Her touch calmed him.

"Millie, I'm convinced that it was fate that brought you to my doorstep. We were meant to meet."

She finally smiled at him and reached out to smooth his hair behind his ear. "I agree."

"This past year with you…I can barely even put it into words. You've made me happier than I ever thought I could be. Then I thought I deserved to be."

"Me too," she murmured, her eyes focused on his mouth like she just wanted him to finish talking so she could have him.

"And I want to feel this way forever. That's why…" He paused to pull something from his pocket. "That's why I'm asking you to be my wife."

Millie stared at him wordlessly, like he was speaking a language she didn't understand, then looked down at the ring clasped in his fingers. "Wait…"

"Millie Jeremy, will you marry me?"

Silence.

Hayden waited as he watched the thoughts take shape in

her head. Expressions flashed across her face—joy, shock, incredulity—until an otherworldly shriek tore out of her.

"YES!"

She leapt up, the blanket forgotten, and threw herself into his arms. Hayden could barely keep himself upright, clutching the ring in one fist while he held the two of them up with the other. Millie covered his face with kisses, and within a few seconds he realized that his fiancée was straddling him, naked in the firelight. Her satiny skin made him long to pull off his own clothing and bury himself inside of her.

"Please put this ring on before you knock it out of my hand," he laughed.

She kept kissing him even as she held her left hand out. Hayden managed to weather the barrage of kisses while putting the thing on her finger. When she felt the weight of it, she paused, her lips still puckered.

Millie turned her hand slowly so the diamond caught light from the fire. Her mouth dropped open.

"How big is this thing?" she asked, her voice filled with awe.

"Big enough that it's got an insurance policy," he laughed. "But all that matters is you like it. I remember you said emerald cut is your favorite."

"It is." She bit her lip as tears filled her eyes, glancing from him to the ring over and over. "I love it. I love it so much."

"I'm glad," he murmured, his lips pressed against her ear. "And you know what I love?"

He didn't give her a chance to answer as he lowered her on top of the blanket, ready to show her exactly what he meant with every inch of his body.

Join Maya Black's Newsletter

Thank you for reading *Snowed in with the Mafia!* If you enjoyed it, I'd appreciate you leaving a review anywhere you can!

If you'd like to join my newsletter you can do so at https://www.subscribepage.com/p3j3r1

What do you get? Inside peeks at covers, help choosing characters, what I'm working on next, and so many more fun items!

See you there!

About Maya Black

Maya Black lives in the Rocky Mountains with her husband and animals and loves being out in nature. She loves all things coffee and books!

She's a new author but has been an avid reader her whole life with stories brewing in her mind. She's finally putting pen to paper to write in a mix of genres but all will include an element of romance.

Join me everywhere you can at https://linktr.ee/authormayablack

Also by Maya Black

ANTHOLOGIES

- Cracked Fairy Tales
- Practical Potions
- Twisted Fairy Tales
- Echoes of the Dead
- Rose of Disgrace
- Evil Hearts - Coming February 2025

STANDALONES

- What Might Have Been
- Yule Spice
- Unchained Melody
- Alice's Illusions
- Wishful Witch
- Bet on Love - Coming April 2025
- Rebel Rose - Coming September 2025
- The Winchester House - Coming October 2025
- Nick's Wish - Coming November 2025
- Bindings, Crimes, & a Chihuahua (Cozy Mystery) - Coming December 2025

SNOWED IN SERIES

Can be read in any order

- Snowed in with the Mafia
- Snowed in with the Billionaire
- Snowed in with the Brother's Best Friend - Coming February 2025
- More coming in Winter 2025/2026

www.ingramcontent.com/pod-product-compliance
Ingram Content Group UK Ltd.
Pitfield, Milton Keynes, MK11 3LW, UK
UKHW022204110125
453409UK00011B/385